THE ORIGINS OF MILLER'S CROSSING

David Clark

CONTENTS

1 4
2 8
3 11
4 16
5 20
6 24
7 28
8 31
9 37
10 40
11 43
12 46
13 49
14 53
15 57
16 60
17 63
18 66
19 69
20 71
21 75
21 79
23 80
24 83
25 88
26 91
27 94
28 98
29 102
30 108

31	111
1	115
Also by David Clark	120
What Did You Think of THE ORIGINS of MILLER'S CROSSING?	122
GET YOUR FREE READERS KIT	123
About the Author	124

1

The newly drawn night brought with it a familiar friend in the form of a dense mist to the 18th century Scottish fishing town of St. Margret's Hope. One might call it fog, but fog does not soak you as you walk through it, like this did. With the disappearance of the last light of day, darkness reigned for a few fleeting hours until the rise of the full moon. The white light from their lunar visitor cast eerie shadows behind every home, stone wall, and hill. In the distance, dogs howled at the object. Other livestock, such as cows and sheep, normally never paid any attention to the moon, but tonight was no normal night.

With a fresh log on the fire, William Miller settled in for the night. Before he headed in, his animals seemed restless. Something not all that uncommon. Many times, an approaching change in the weather was to blame. When night fell, the restlessness became worse. They were not overly vocal, with long mournful calls. Their calls were short and stressed, and they were not still. From inside his stone home, he heard them, but ignored them. He told himself they would settle down, but the crash he heard out in their pen told a different story.

William slid his feet into his brown hide boots, and grabbed his grey sporran. After a long bout with wolves two summers ago, William and his neighbor, John Sanders, came up with the idea to keep a sporran packed with rocks to grab in a hurry. He pulled two rocks out to have at the ready as he threw open his door. He ran to the pen, with every expectation of finding one or two wolves roaming around, or maybe a stray dog from one of the neighboring farms. A chill went up the back of his neck, and he dropped the rocks to the ground and put his hands on his hips.

"You should be used to them by now," he said to the animals. The 'them' he spoke of were three flickering human forms that roamed across his pasture a few hundred yards away from his livestock. William watched them. Instead of moving straight across and away, they wandered and meandered here and there. The 'theres' were further away from him and his livestock, but the 'heres' brought them close.

When they reached the edge of his land, they circled back instead of crossing through. William knew this would continue for the rest of the night if he did not put a stop to it. He walked out to greet them and stopped right in their path. Two of them moved around him. The third went right through. In all outward appearance, they didn't even know he was there. The cold icy chill from being passed through was a sensation that William never got used to, no matter how many times it had happened. Feeling one's internal organs shiver and shake was as close to death he could go without dying himself.

"Now, just go on and leave. No need to cause any trouble here," William said. All three continued to walk away from him. He hadn't got their attention. Reaching into his sporran. He retrieved a single rock and then tossed it at the three specters. It passed straight through the middle one and prompted no reaction. "That never works," William said under his breath. It was true, that never worked. Simple actions, like talking, rarely did. He could count the number of times it had on one hand. But he had to hope. It was a better option than what he usually did.

"Ya! Ya!", he yelled as he ran toward them from behind. When he reached them, he zigzagged through them, over and over again. The first pass through never got their attention. They would keep moving, just as these did, but if he did it enough, they would notice and move away from him. The only question was, could he stand the ice-cold grip he felt every time he did.

On the third pass, the one on the right took notice. A weathered old gentleman, with a wrinkled face and straggly white hair, turned toward William. The empty sockets he had for eyes followed William as he danced around them in an attempt to herd them like a sheep dog. It was working. They moved straight across to the other side. William's movements cut them off each time they tried to turn. If they ignored him, he ran through them to remind him of his presence. Each time he did so, their demeanor changed. The pleasant chaps on a nice stroll through his pasture were now rather irritated. Their hollow eyes, and the scowls on their faces, watched him. The mouths moved on two of them, as if they attempted to lecture or warn him, but nothing came out.

This dance continued across his land, and across the trail that separated his and the next, but he didn't stop. He wanted to make sure they didn't come back that night. He continued on until he felt they were far enough away from his farm to cause any trouble. If they caused anyone else trouble, that was none of his concern. His goal was a good night's sleep. There wasn't much of the night left, but at least it would be peaceful.

He bid his ghastly friends adieu and bowed as they passed by. When he stood up, he came face to face with the weathered old man that had taken an interest in him. The man reached out with his flickering arm of blue mist and grabbed him by the back of the neck. Its icy touch felt like a thousand pins pricking the surface of his skin. The man leaned forward and contorted its face to twice its normal size and screamed right at him. This was a sound that William heard, there was no mistaking it. William screamed in response, and fell backwards onto the damp grass as the three continued on and disappeared into the mist.

"William, is that you?", asked a sleepy John Sanders. William's neighbor approached. He held a single candle lantern as he scanned the dark fog-covered ground with his eyes. He was two years younger than William, but had a wife and two strapping boys, ages five and seven.

"Ya, over here."

It was only a few seconds before John's lantern illuminated William's form on the ground. John extended a hand and helped his lifelong friend up onto his feet. William pulled at his shirt and kilt, now both soaked from the moisture on the ground.

"What are you doing out here, and what was all that yelling?"

"Didn't you hear it?", William asked.

"Hear what?", John responded. "All I heard was you. Screaming your bloody head off, like you were some wild dog or wolf. What was all that about?"

Still pulling the cold wet clothing away from his already chilled body, William didn't say anything. He didn't need to. The sheepish look on his face said it all.

"Again?"

"Three of them," he said, as he held up three fingers in the candlelight to drive the point home.

"Three?", asked a weary John.

A quick nod from William answered the question of his friend and neighbor.

John looked to either side of them, and then turned around to look behind him. His sleepy eyes peered into the dark, but saw nothing. "You sure?"

"Yes."

"Where are they?"

William threw his hands up, and looked at his friend. His eyebrows raised to cap the question marks in his eyes. "I lost track when I fell down."

John turned around and headed back toward his farmhouse. The circle of light that had encircled both of them receded and followed him. William found himself once again in the dark cool fog of the still night. "Go home, William. It's a good thing I have been your friend for so long and understand. Someone else might think you aren't right in the head. Chained up in some asylum is where you'd be."

William knew what he said was true. He had hidden this side of him from everyone, except John. John only knew because the truth was the only way to explain how he was acting. They were friends for as long as they could remember. Anytime they weren't doing chores, or helping out on the farm, they could be found along the simple stone wall that separated their families properties. Probably up to no good. Many a day in their younger years was spent throwing small pebbles at birds and bugs. As they got older, they graduated to talking about girls, and plans to get out of this place. Sometimes they spent the afternoon taking sips out of a swiped jug of William's father's homemade whiskey, while talking of all the girls they never had the nerve to talk to.

One early evening, after they were about a third of a jug deep, William had John hide the jug behind the wall. He'd seen a man walking toward them. John had done as he was asked, but questioned him. He didn't see the man, and insisted he wasn't there at all. John suggested William had more than his share of the whiskey. The closer the man came, the weirder William felt. He started to doubt his eyes and believed John had a point. Maybe he had had a bit too much that night. A cold sweat had developed on his neck, and pins prickled up and down his spine.

It wasn't long until William got a better look at the man. He flashed and flickered. There one second, and gone the next. Combined with the feeling that had come over his body, disbelief had set in. He rubbed both eyes hard with his hands. Each eyelid burped silently as he rubbed hard enough to force tears out the sides. When he opened them again, he was still there, and now closer than before.

William hopped down off the wall and walked out to meet him. It didn't take long for him to realize he could see straight through the man. When he reached him, he circled him as he continued to walk. The man paid no attention to William. Attempts to talk to him went ignored. When William reached out to tap him on the shoulder, he about passed out when his fingers went straight through the man's shoulder.

John accused him of putting him on, but after more and more occurrences of this with William over the years, he began to accept the truth, no matter out outlandish it was. His friend could see ghosts.

"See you in the morning, John," William called after his friend.

John held up the lantern and grunted as he continued back to his house.

William started his trek home. He took a look around every once in a while. It was just out of curiosity though; he knew he wouldn't see anything. The feeling he always had when they were around was gone. A quick hop up and over the same stone wall he and John had spent many an afternoon at when they were younger, put him back on his land. His home wasn't much further, which was good. The cold damp air, combined with his wet clothes created quite a chill in his bones. He passed his animal pen on the way to his farmhouse. They were all sleeping. No longer disturbed. That was good. William was tired, and wasn't in the mood to hear them all night.

2

The midday sun chased away the fog of night. This was a daily battle. One that both sides won from time to time. If a score was kept, the North Sea would claim victory, with many a day seeing overcast clouds or dense fog for the entirety, denying the ground the warmth of sunlight. This contributed to the lush green hills that overlooked the stone buildings that lined the coast, and made good land for farming, one of two main professions in the village. You either farmed, or fished.

William and John farmed. Partially because that was what their families did. William had two uncles that fished, and his grandfather did for a bit before settling on farming. He tried it once with one of his uncles when he was only thirteen. One shouldn't really say only thirteen. At that age you are expected to start learning your trade. The decision of what that would be was one William had not made yet. The sea called to him. It would be cliché to call its image romantic, but to him it was magical. Every day boats headed out, and every night the fog rolled in. Then, one by one, the glimmer of a lantern hanging on the bow peered through the dense marine layer as each of the boats returned with their crew and their catch. Dozens of people rushed the wharf to assist in offloading the haul. Everyone worked well past the fall of darkness, until the work was done. Then they all retired to a local pub to share in drink, food, more drink, grand stories, and even more drink.

Farmers, well, farmed.

His uncle, Logan Miller, offered to take him out with his crew to show him the ropes one day. William didn't hesitate to ask his father before he jumped at it. No concern was given to any disappointment or rejection his father may have felt for his rush to consider a different path.

It was a rather calm day, but being the first time William had ever been on a boat of any type, he had no sea legs, and struggled to keep both his balance and his last meal. The former he lost more than the latter. There was more to the profession than he had expected. Tons of preparation, handled by the two youngest members of the crew, Harris Lonston and Oliver Walling. Both a mere two months older than himself, by the calendar, but their time on board had produced two burly men. Harris, with long locks of red hair, and Oliver, with a mass of dark hair. Their job, was everything but actual fishing. They cut bait, ensured all hooks were baited and ready. When one of the four others on board called "hook", both would run to that man's side. Each stood waiting with large metal hooks in their hands. Once the fish was at the side of the boat, they reached over and thrust the points of the hooks into the shiny-scaled side of the fish. With a single move, they heaved the fish up over the railing and onto the deck. William's uncle then took control of the fish. He cut, gutted, and filleted, right there on the boat. The head and the guts were thrown back overboard, with bits reused for bait. Logan explained to William that he did this by himself, as he didn't trust anyone else not to over-cut the fish, robbing them of usable weight.

William had taken his turn at cutting bait and loading the hooks. It hadn't taken long for him to get into a rhythm, despite the smell. On one occasion, he turned, with both hands holding bits of fish for the hooks, and felt a tingle along the back of his neck. Not wanting to lose what was left of his last meal in front of everyone, he steadied his legs and swallowed hard to bury the feeling. It didn't go away. It intensified. When he rounded the main mast, he ran face to face into the image of an old white-haired man, skin weathered and waterlogged. His stare blank, and mouth mumbling without making a sound.

"Boy, you ok?", asked Finlay Leigh, a large mass of a man who spent much of the trip sharing jokes with his uncle, most of which went straight over William's head. He would have to trust the thundering laughs that erupted from each of the men as a sign that they were funny. William saw Finlay looking at him through the old man. This was not the first time William had seen a ghost, not by a long shot, but it was the worst time possible. He wanted to show he was strong and capable. These men wouldn't understand. If he tried to tell them, it would be an end to his time onboard.

"Yep," he said, as strong and stout as he could muster. Maybe even overdoing it a bit. William stepped through the man, and brushed off the cold chill so no one would notice.

As the afternoon waned, the sea showed more of its character. Storms formed along the horizon and headed their way. Just the simple task of walking took on a new challenge. The deck rose to meet, or dropped away from, every step. When he didn't have to move, he stayed clamped to the railing with his eyes locked on the center of the ship. The others moved with ease. They seemed to enjoy the extra challenge, along with the spray of water over every exterior edge.

There was no concern on anyone's face, except William's, until the boat rocked to port under the edge of a wave. The water washed over the deck sending everyone sprawling on the wooden planks. Loose buckets, line, and hooks, were last seen going over the starboard side.

"Put into the waves!" yelled Finlay.

"It is. They are coming from all sides!" responded Logan, from the helm.

From where William sat, he could confirm what his uncle had said. He felt the boat rocking forward and back in the waves, while others hit them on the broadsides, sending the boat twisting from side to side. His uncle stood stone-still and locked onto the scene ahead of them. His arms turned the wheel to trace the path his brain had mapped through each of the approaching waves. Harris and Oliver had taken up positions similar to William. The child in each of them emerged above their more mature exteriors. They trembled, eyes darting from side to side at the crash of each wave.

That was the last William saw of them, at least onboard the boat. A single crash rolled it over, the sail and mast both submerged in another wave that had approached from the opposite side. Cracks and pops thundered all around them, but it was not from the storm. Large beams of cedar were giving way under the great strain, signaling the beginning of the end.

The only other sound William remembered hearing, other than the sound of the wind, the stinging rain, and the boat breaking apart, was a single laugh and bellow from Finlay, "She's ah going to win this one fellows."

William didn't remember when he went into the water. Nor did he remember how the rest of the boat broke up. He knew the section of railing he had hung onto was still tight in his grasp when he made it to the surface. If it hadn't been for that section of wood, he was sure he would be on his way to the bottom. Instead, they both floated up to the surface and rode the waves of the tempest.

The waves outlasted the wind and rain. It was at the crest of one of those towering waves that William saw how close to the shore he was. He kicked hard, and hung on to his savior. Up and down the waves they went, until he reached a point where each of the waves rushed toward the shore, giving him a welcome push. The last crash of the wave sent him flipping head over ass onto the beach

After that day, William continued to see Harris, Oliver, Finlay, and his uncle from time to time strolling through town aimlessly. Each time he sees one of them serves as a reminder that being a farmer wasn't a bad way to make a living.

3

"William, you ready?", John yelled from outside. He was standing next to a cart hitched to his faithful burro, the most useful tool on his own farm. That burro not only pulled the cart to town, but pulled the plow in the field, hauled loads across the property, and anything else John needed him to do. William had one too, but being a bit older, it was best used for the jobs around the farm, not for trips to town.

"Yep," he said as he emerged out the door of the smokehouse with three large slabs of cured pork. "One more," he said, and dropped the meat down on an empty spot in the cart. Back into the smokehouse he went, but he re-emerged quickly, this time with two large chunks of pork belly. "Last pig of the season for me. The others have to plump up a bit." A quick look back at his animal pen caused a grunt from the three hogs that remained. It was as if they knew they were the topic of the conversation.

The two men walked to town, as they had more times than they could remember. Many times, alongside their fathers as they led a burro, or sometimes a horse, that pulled a cart behind them. For the past ten years, it was their turn to lead the cart, their responsibility, and their lives. The conversation during these trips hadn't changed much through the years. The topic was always the same, dreams. They each dreamed of something bigger.

John wanted to expand the family farm, an idea he had been pitching to his father since he was only nine. Something he felt would force his father to see him as grownup, no longer a child. Instead, his father had brushed it off as just that, a childish dream. "You don't understand how much work it takes to keep up what we have," he always said. Even now, John still dreamed of doing just that.

The dreams William had were loftier. He was a farmer, only because the other option was, well, less attractive. Farming was less likely to take his life. Of course, there are still dozens of ways you could die on the farm. The thought of leaving Saint Margaret's Hope was one he couldn't remember where it came from. No one had ever mentioned anything about leaving to him. There were no encounters with strange or mysterious individuals who told tales of the outside world. It was just a thought. One that he spent many an afternoon sitting on top of the cliff imagining. His gaze looking out over the ocean at nothing in particular, while his mind pondered what was out there.

Meadows and horse tracks gave way to sparse buildings and cobblestone walks as they crept closer to town. The shoes of the burro, and the wheels of the cart that were silent on the dirt and grass path, now clattered and clopped on the stones. The midday sun may have chased the mist away for the moment, but the cool air still hung around. The walk in did not exert either of the young men, yet William still reached up to wipe a few beads of cold sweat off the back of his neck and his brow. John noticed this, and an obvious lack of color in his friend's face. "Is one of your friends around?"

"No!", William snapped back.

"You sure? You look sick." John then followed the path of William's eyes, and said with a bit of a sneer. "Good day, Ainslee."

"Good day, John, William. Heading to town?"

John looked at William. The color was gone from his face. You would think he had seen a ghost, but that was really not something that would spook him. This situation, on the other hand, was something different. Something that petrified William. With raised eyebrows, John tried to encourage William to speak. Instead, he was a statue. Frozen expression and all. With no sign of hope that William would come around, John gave up and responded, "Yes. Market day."

"I will be in town later. Maybe I will see you around."

"Maybe so," John said. He nudged the burro in the side, and they started forward again. Out of the corner of his eye, he watched William, to make sure he didn't need to give him a nudge too. He didn't, William was moving all on his own, shoulders slumped and slack jawed.

Before they had passed the end of the stone fence that surrounded the large two story cobblestone estate, they were greeted again. This time by a middle aged man, someone who would be their fathers' age, in fact, he was a close friend of their fathers'. Deep character lines on his face hinted at the years spent at sea, but his waist coat and buckled brogues told a different story, something more provincial.

"Good day, boys. Going to market?"

"Good day, Lord McLayer," they both said.

"Yes sir. I have fresh turnips and root, you need any?", offered John.

"That I might. You two have a good day."

When the two were clear of the estate, John cut William a look. There was no doubt William saw it. There was a reply look shared between the two friends.

"What was that about?"

William returned the look again.

"You can talk to Lord McLayer, but can't utter a sound to his daughter?"

William didn't have a reply. Not one that would explain the situation. It was something he didn't quite understand either. Ainslee McLayer was their age. He and John had been around her for years. Several years ago, he found himself feeling more nervous around her than before. More aware of anything he may have done embarrassing. A comment, joke, or anything else that made him appear less refined, and more like a child, sent a dagger through his soul. John had noticed it too. It was hard for him not to. There were activities that William would not take part of when she was around. Something as simple as skipping a rock across a pond on the back acre of his father's farm was an activity William avoided when Ainslee was near. John would rib him about it in front of her, which always drew his ire in the form of a look or a comment.

All he knew was, anytime he caught her green eyes and rosy cheeks framed by her flowing red hair, every ounce of confidence drained from his body, and he hated it. She had been, was, is, a great friend. He fancied her, and at one point considered courting her. It would never be permitted though; she was royalty, and he was just a farmer. Not to mention, why would she even consider him? The life he could offer her would be so far below her station.

The two made it to town. The first stop was at the butcher's, to sell the slabs of pork and chunks of pork belly. William had promised him that sow a few weeks prior. Mr. Arlen saw it during a visit out to see William. He had done business with his father, and made a point to visit their farm, and several of his other regular suppliers to check out his future supplies. When he spied the animal during a recent visit, his hands shaped the cuts his brain was making, while his eyes took in the beauty of the beast.

The payment for the meat was a bag with a few coins, but that wasn't the most valuable to William. Not that he didn't need them. He needed to purchase the few other supplies he didn't have means to provide for on the farm. Oh, and bread. He had meal and wheat on his farm, but not the talent to create a fluffy loaf with a hard crust. His attempts always produced something that resembled a field stone. The commodity he received, that held the true value to William, was the five pounds of tender beef steak Mr. Arlen had wrapped up waiting for him. A real treat. His mouth watered just thinking about throwing a hunk of that on the fire when he returned home. The rest would be salted and hung in the cellar to dry. That would have to wait, William and John had a few other items to take care of in town first. John still needed to sell the bushels of turnips and parsley loaded in the back of the cart.

On Front Street, just along the wharf, stood a public market. There were no booths or buildings that made it anything official. Just dozens of people gathered with their goods to sell. It had started as a place to buy fish from the local fleet. One by one, farmers tested their luck and wheeled in a load of their freshest crop. No one remembers who the first one was, but it didn't take long before each of the major farms in the area were regulars. No one complained. It was a win-win for everyone.

John directed the burro into an empty space. Using a stone, he blocked the wheels to keep them from rolling down the slight incline on the road. The cart itself leaned down a little toward the back, to create the perfect display for his goods.

"Keep an eye on it?", John asked.

William just nodded. It wasn't a big ask, nor one he was unfamiliar with. This was the same routine every week. With the cart in place, William watched it to make sure it didn't roll any, while John unhitched the burro and walked him over to a water trough surrounded by green grass. This may have seemed common sense, but as with much the two of them had learned in their endeavors, they had learned this particular skill the hard way. Neither had paid too much attention to what their father's did on the trips into town. Instead, they ran through the market with their friends in town. Many times, their fathers had to waste several minutes at the end of each day searching for the whereabouts of their sons. They would be found running in the streets, sitting on the wharf as they watched the fleet come in, or at any of the three or more friends they had made in town on such previous trips.

They should have paid better attention during those many trips. Each lost their father at a young age. The winter of 1710 was a bad one. Storm after storm blew in from the coast. The wind, rain, and cold were relentless. At times it wouldn't let up for weeks. The problem with being a farmer was, neither the animals nor the crops cared about the weather. Both needed to be tended to. This invited in the other thing that blew in with the storm, the creep. That is what his mom had called it. The type of cough that crept in and stayed. Started as just a hack here and a hack there, but got worse over time, until it was all the time. Those that could afford visits to the town surgeon were given herbs and liniments. Not that they did any good. The coughing continued until life left them. First, his mother, and then, three weeks later, his father. That last week was filled with tasks around the farm, while his father directed from the house. This was the first time William was responsible for the farm. John's parents followed in the coming months. Both boys were traumatized by the loss of their parents. William more than John. John never saw the ghosts of his parents around the farm. Something William did on more than one occasion. At times it warmed his heart, but at others, it chilled it.

Of the many things their fathers had taught them during their dying days, how to secure the cart wasn't one of them. Maybe it was something they had assumed wasn't needed, since the boys had accompanied them on many trips into town. It didn't happen on their first trip in, or even their second. Something that William believed now was just dumb luck. On the third trip, they leaned the cart downward, like both boys remembered seeing their fathers do, as well as everyone else there. When John unhitched the burro, William's eyes exploded before his mouth screamed. The cart started to roll down the incline, gathering speed the whole way. Everyone stood and watched as it rolled through the market. No one laughed, even though both boys later thought the image of a cart loaded with turnips, wheat, and roots rolling down the road was humorous. It avoided any other carts and people, but caromed back and forth between a few buildings before it tipped over on its side. What remained of their crops fell onto the ground with a flop. The rest was scattered up the road, tracing their path. Even with that calamity, they still managed to sell everything they brought. William believed people bought from them because they felt sorry for them. For the loss of their parents, and their inability to do something as simple as chock the wheels of a cart.

4

With both the cart and burro secured, William left John to his bartering. There was no set price for anything, just what the buyer wanted to pay, and what the seller was willing to accept. William had no patience for such things. One reason, he wasn't very good at it. John got on him all the time for offering too much and accepting too little. Something William just waved off.

Much like he used to as a young boy, William wandered the streets. It was not an aimless wander, as he followed the same path he had for some years. The destination was always the same. It wasn't the Lion's Pub just off the corner of Front Street. a popular stop for many after a long day at the market, but not for William. His endpoint was the same as it had been since he was eight. A spot with a rock that stuck out a tad higher than all the rest. Perfect for sitting. The view was the wide open ocean. Not a view of the harbor, mind you. After his one experience, there was no pining for days out fishing. This was more pining for what else was out there. Out there beyond the dark blue expanse and cloudy skies with the occasional patch of blue. What did the rest of the world look like? Was it like here? Meadows of lush green, dotted with stone-walled homes? He didn't know. Not many in St. Margaret's Hope did. He couldn't remember the last time any visitor from anywhere else had wandered into town.

William spent hours upon hours on that rock lost in thought. Nothing distracted him. Not the white birds that swirled around hoping he had a morsel of food to share. Not the people that walked past, that at times, paused to look at him with a curious gaze. This occurred more now than it did when he was younger. It wasn't an odd sight to see a child sitting on a rock looking out at nothing, but a grown man was something different.

"Um hum," coughed a delicate voice behind him. A light shadow now shed over William's back.

"Um hum," again. William didn't stir.

This time there was no cough to get his attention, it was a tap on the shoulder that sent William spinning around and grabbing at the rock to avoid an embarrassing tumble into the water below.

"Relax," said the voice.

William steadied himself and wiped the fear created sweat from his forehead. He looked up and saw the vision of an angel standing over him. The sun haloed around flowing locks of curly red hair. The voice that asked him to relax, was the sweetest sound he had ever heard. His eyes adjusted to the sun as the angel sat on the rock next to him. Her cherub face came clearly into view. Green eyes, rosy cheeks, and perfect lips.

"Do you see what you are looking for?", asked Ainslee. Her hand met his on the rock, sending a little flutter through his heart. That would be the second time today she had done that to him.

"Nah," he said. His gaze moved from her, back to the open ocean.

"What do you think is out there? You, more than anyone I know, have dreamt of leaving."

"I honestly don't know. I just feel there is something greater planned for me than this. If there is, it has to be out there." This was something William had felt for as long as he could remember. It was also something he had once asked his father about. His father hadn't agreed or disagreed. Instead, he told William, "God has a purpose for us all. Our job is to find it and do it the best we can, in the service of our lord."

The local priest, Father Henry laughed, when the precocious ten year old boy asked him about it after a Sunday sermon. "My son, you are far too young to worry about such things. When it is time for you to know your purpose, you will know." The cheery, and cheeky, priest patted him on the head and sent him on his way to play with the other kids while he talked with their parents, but even then, William knew he was different. He hadn't seen any ghosts yet, but he had felt something. A sensation, and desire, that he couldn't put his finger on. What he did know, whatever it was, wasn't here in St. Margaret's Hope.

"Why didn't you talk to me earlier?", asked Ainslee.

"Your dad was there," William said. His head dropped, and his eyes stared at the rock next to where he sat.

Even with her face skewed into the cock-eyed expression she gave him; she was still a vision of beauty. Two quick, but soft, pats on his hand remind him of the warmth of her touch. The cold north wind invaded the space left each time she lifted her hand up. The feeling was a comfort, and he knew she meant it as such. She had done it before. Usually just before she said, and there it was, "He is just a man. He respected your father. He will, he does, respect you."

"I am just a farmer," said William. This was the same response he had given several times before.

"You need to stop that. That is honorable work."

William just shook his head. She didn't understand at all. It had nothing to do with honorable work or not. Ainslee deserved a life he knew there was no way a farmer could provide. Of course, that wasn't the biggest obstacle in his way. There was still that talk. The talk that terrified him more than any ghost he had encountered, and more than the thought of going out for another fishing trip. There was no way, Lord Sheamus McLayer, the town elder and largest landowner, would ever give his daughter's hand to a farmer.

This was a dance his mind had played over and over for years. Each time, the steps still led to the same result. Which was why neither he nor Ainslee had let John, or anyone else, know they were a little more than just two people who waved awkwardly at each other. They both understood each other, but what William also understood was, it couldn't be.

She wrapped her petite hand around his and said, "Let's take a walk."

"What? Here?", he asked. His eyes were wide open, and he scanned around for anyone that might see them.

"Sure, why not? Just up the road a bit." She wasn't taking no from him, and stood up, pulling his hand with hers. One thing William had learned, once she set her mind on something, he couldn't change it.

They walked hand in hand. She strolled confidently next to him. Their hands swung between them. William wasn't as confident. There was no denying he liked how it felt, but that was overshadowed by the worry of the wrong person seeing them. He didn't know what would happen, but he knew he didn't want to find out.

The further they walked without passing anyone, that fear melted away slightly. So much so, he didn't notice that she had led him another three streets further than just up the road, as she had said. Past the pub. Past the town center, which was still empty, and up toward the church.

In fact, William was so lost in the bliss of the moment, his skin jumped when the words, "Good day, Father," escaped out of Ainslee's lips. The fear that accompanied those words forced his head down and his eyes to the ground. At some point he would need to look up and greet her father eye to eye, he knew that. He also knew such public displays of affection, even something so simple, without the father's permission, was not looked upon with approval.

"Ainslee, William," said a comforting and aged voice.

The ball of nerves that had squeezed his insides down to a tight and painful speck the size of a pea had loosened slightly. His head rose slowly, as the tension in the muscles of his neck loosened. Black mud-stained shoes were topped by a black cassock that hung loosely on the thin man. At the top, a simple white collar stood out against the black garb. The man's wrinkled and age-spotted hands were folded neatly in front of him. His weathered face and steel blue eyes smiled at the two below his black wide-brimmed hat.

"Good day, Father," William said as he greeted Father Logan Henry.

"Nice day for a walk," he said.

Ainslee said, "Yes, it is, Father." She held up their combined hands a little higher as if to make sure he saw, and they continued down the road. There was a little more of a hop to her step than there had been.

William, on the other hand, felt his shoulders slump as they walked away, and Ainslee felt it. She also knew why. "No need to worry. He won't tell anyone. Trust me," she said, as her hand gave his two quick squeezes.

5

Flames flickered in the fire and seared the remains of the fat that dripped on the grate, while also providing warmth. The aromas of cooked salted beef still wafted around his home. William sat back in his father's chair while he drank ale from his father's tin mug. No matter how long his father had been gone, William still saw everything as his father's. Well, not everything. Thanks to a spooked goat, William had to rebuild the pen, so he guessed the pen was his. The table in the drying house was his, too. Even though it wasn't much more than a large stump he cut from a tree downed by lightning on the back corner of the farm. It had sat there for months after it fell. When William cut into a sick hen, he knew he needed a new cutting table. It was bad luck, and bad health, to use the same table again after you butchered a sick animal.

He knew how to make a table. Basic carpentry was a necessary skill his father had taught him. It was also something William enjoyed, but that was when he had the time to do it right. Time was something he didn't have an abundance of on the farm, so the tree seemed like a good solution. The time lying on the ground had allowed it to dry out, which made cutting a large section of the trunk free not a difficult task. Getting it back to the farm was a different story. Its girth was too wide to fit between the sides of his cart. Probably a relief to the horse he had attached to the front. The ground was wet, and the first attempts to drag it had done nothing more than chew up a streak of earth. Again, his horse felt a great sense of relief as he walked him back to his stall. William then faced the last option he had. With the help of the horse before he walked him back to the stall, he tipped the mass of wood up on its end. The section he cut was a three-foot-thick section of the five-foot-wide trunk, and it was round.

With a hard push, the mass of wood rocked forward and then rocked back. Another shove, this time a little harder, sent it rolling forward by about a half a rotation. A third push, a little harder, resulted in the same outcome. Push after push, some harder than the others, to get it up and over an uneven patch of ground here, or out of a hole there, and the stump rolled closer to his home. It took him a few minutes to figure out how to turn it, but he managed that as well. After several hours, he stood exhausted in front of the drying shed and faced a question. Would it fit through the door? That was a question he had never considered when he cut the massive trunk. He eyeballed it a few times and lined it up. With his eyes closed and ears braced for a crash, he gave it a mighty shove. The crash never came. Instead, it rolled forward and through the door, with no issue. William centered it in the room and then pushed it over with a thud. Even as tired as he was, he felt a satisfaction unlike any he had felt before.

He felt a little of that satisfaction as he sat there at the table drinking his ale. Was it the tasty steak he traded for in town and cooked when he got home, or was it the time he spent with Ainslee? He wasn't sure. What was clear was, any dreams or thoughts of the latter needed to be put out of his mind. There was no future there. Every attempt Ainslee made to convince him otherwise just prolonged the inevitable.

Screams, shouts, and the wild neighing of a horse invaded his deep pondering and snapped William from his momentary pleasure. He sat straight up and listened to the sounds. They were not coming from his animals. That much was clear, but he still sprang up to go check. Each were quiet in their pen, unaffected by the sounds. They were far away, but not that far. It had to be one of the neighboring farms. He peered into the darkness. There, just visible in the settling fog, were spots of light. The lanterns danced in the distance as the yelling continued. William started in that direction, to lend assistance.

As he got closer, he could make out two figures, each with a lantern, moving back and forth frantically. The yelling and shouting he heard surrounded other phrases that he was now able to make out in the distance.

"Father, I tell you...there is something ungodly around. I can feel it in my bones."

William heard no reply, but assumed the voice he recognized as his neighbor, Gerald Boyd, was talking to the other person out with him, holding a lantern. The lanterns, which had started as just specks of lights, were now globes of lights, inside William saw the figures of two men as they rushed from spot to spot around Gerald's stables. He waited until he was closer before he called out, "Gerald, everything ok?"

Both globes of light stopped in their tracks. Both figures inside the globes turned toward William as he approached. He felt the quick pinch of pins pricking the skin on the back of his neck. The sensation left, but was replaced by several beads of a cold sweat. He now felt in his bones the same thing Gerald did.

"William, is that you?"

"Yes, Gerald. Everything ok? I heard the yelling."

The globe to the left walked out to meet William, while the one to the right continued a search for something in the stable. As Gerald's face came into view, his hand jutted out to greet his neighbor. He took it and gave it a firm shake. William could feel a tremble in his friend's grip. It was also visible in his face. "What is the trouble?" he asked.

"Something has the animals spooked. I have never heard them make these sounds before."

William offered a possible cause, "Is it a fox or snake?"

That suggestion was met with a quick shake of Gerald's head. He pulled him close and said, "It is not something of this world. I know it."

"Oh, come on. I am sure it is just another animal. Let's have a look." William may have brushed the notion off, but that was just to calm his friend. He knew Gerald's feeling to be true. He felt it, and it grew stronger with every step he took toward the stable. As he walked closer, he recognized the other individual to be Father Henry. He searched the stable at a furious pace, with a disturbed look on his face.

"Father."

"William, I would stand back. Something is not right here."

William didn't heed the warning and kept walking forward.

"William," Father Henry began, before he turned his head to look at him. His eyes delivered the message more than the words, "I am serious. I would stay back."

William knew darn well he couldn't do that. Not because he was stubborn, but because he already saw the problem. There was a single flickering spirit roaming between the stalls. It looked to be that of a young girl. Her face was empty and soulless, like they all were, but something about her demeanor told him she was lost, or had lost something. Something that held a strong connection to her. He often wondered if the locations he saw them in had something to do with their past life. In this instance, maybe she gravitated to the stable because she had had a horse when she was alive. Of course, that never explained those he found just roaming around an open field, or trapped in a wall between two rooms. It was just a theory.

"Does your colt kick?" he asked, as he followed her toward a stall. He could see right away what spooked the animals. She was passing straight through them. The cold shiver he had felt in the past when that happened was enough to spook him.

"He rears up, but hasn't ever kicked with his backs before," said Gerald.

The word "before", stuck in his head. It didn't mean he never would, just hadn't yet, and William didn't really want to be around, or anywhere near him, when it happened for the first time. He kept his eyes on the beast as he reached over the wood door and undid the tie.

"William, wait!" exclaimed Father Henry.

"No time, Father. I am pretty good with animals. Just give me a second." William crept open the door with slow movements, so as to not spook the animal any more than it already had been. She was over in the corner, but headed back toward the colt. He knew if he was going to stop this, he was going to have to test the statement Gerald had made about kicking. He reached out to touch the colt and give him some comfort, and also to make sure he knew he was there behind him.

The girl flickered in and out of existence as she walked toward the horse's hind quarters. William positioned himself between them. This would either work, or he would find out if the horse kicked. The girl ran into him. The cold feeling caused his body to shiver, which ran up his arm and to the back side of the horse. It stayed calm, except for just a little jostle forward. The girl stopped and turned away from William. She flickered a few more times, and then disappeared through the wall of the stable. At that moment, the muscles in the beast behind him relaxed, and the various noises throughout the stable subsided.

William waited a few moments before he exited the stall. Father Henry and Gerald waited for him outside. They still held their lanterns, but instead of holding them up around their heads as they searched, each now let the lantern dangle at the end of their arm.

"What was that?" asked Gerald.

William shrugged his shoulders and scratched his head, "Don't know. Whatever it was is gone. He just needed help settling down. They should be fine now."

Father Henry stood there, mouth dropped open, as William walked by him and out into the stable.

He kept walking beyond the large barn door entrance to the stable, and out into the dense fog that hung above the open pasture that was between his farmhouse and Gerald's. "You should be fine for the rest of the night. Night, Gerald. Night, Father."

6

A light breeze blew across the meadow. Its strength was enough to move the coolness from the ocean inland as far as the farmlands, but that didn't help William. Sweat still dripped from his brow and arms. It was possible his horse felt more relief from it, but he didn't know. Both were out in the field, plowing up the remains of his turnip and potato crops. It was time for the late summer planting, and the soil needed to be turned and crops rotated. Where he had grown potatoes would now be turnips and snap bean vines. Where the turnips were, potatoes would be planted.

This was a three day job. William knew that. It always seemed longer each time they finished a row and turned to give him a full view of the untouched ground ahead of them. He didn't complain, neither did the horse, it was what had to be done. Not that there was anyone for him to complain to, the closest person was acres away, doing the same on their property. There wasn't anyone for the horse to complain to either, except William, but the five year old brown and white beast knew that wouldn't do any good.

The pair turned onto their sixth row of the day and started on their seventh. Both were heads down with their task. The horse pulled, while William steered the blade. Grey and white hooded crows circled overhead. Their eyes kept watch over the freshly churned ground for the sign of any insects, worms, or nice juicy grubs that may have been disturbed and pulled to the top. The rattle of the chains and the creak of the wood plow frame buried the sounds of the caws from the birds. It also blocked out the attempt of a visitor to call out to William. The individual made several attempts while he walked across the pasture, but it was only when he and the horse turned to start the eighth row, that William saw him.

"William?"

"Whoa!", William called out to the horse, though it wasn't necessary. The pressure he applied to the yoke had already stopped it. He dropped the leather straps and walked to greet Father Henry as he approached.

"Father, to what do I owe the pleasure?"

"It's that time of year. Looks like you made a lot of progress today," he said as he looked around. Father Henry was sans the normal cassock he wore in and around the church. On this day, he wore black cotton pants, a jacket with a shirt and white collar under it, and a wide brimmed black hat. His choice of footwear were the same mud-stained leather boots he always wore. It was a good thing too. The pasture he had stomped through was just barely drier than a bog, and would have no doubt ruined anything of quality.

"I have, but so much to go. Might need you to do one of those blessing of the crops you do for the Lyle's." William referred to a prayer that the priest had done at a farm over the hill three seasons ago. He had walked around and recited a prayer while he sprinkled holy water in each of the corners. Nobody knows for sure if it worked or not, but the bumper crop that season had made it a legend.

"Eh," the priest waved his hand to the side, "that was just to quiet him. It was something I made up."

William opened his mouth to point out the success they'd felt, but Father Henry held up his hand before he could begin. "Don't say it. Nothing to do with it, my boy. Nothing to do with it. That was the first year he rotated and spread manure around. Lawlyer finally figured out how to farm. That is not why I am here."

"Okay, Father, why are you here?", asked William. He used the back of his hand to wipe his forehead. Sweat continued to pour due to the exertion. Little did he know, there was a smidge of dirt on the back of his hand, and it was now smeared above his eyes. Father Henry saw it, but was way too polite to say anything.

"Last night. I am here about last night," Father Henry said. His voice wavered, and his eyes avoided contact with William's.

"What about last night?", William watched the priest shift his weight back and forth as he made every attempt to avoid eye contact with him. He gave off every appearance of a man that needed to talk about a topic he didn't want to.

"How... Well, William...," Father Henry started and stopped several times before he managed to get the question that was in his head into words. "That was some fine work last night. How did you do it?"

"I am not sure what you mean, Father. The colt was---," Father Henry interrupted William with a wave of his hand.

"Don't tell me you walked into the stall and calmed the colt down. Gerald may believe that, but I don't. Now tell me, what did you see?"

Father Henry was digging for something, William knew that. The question that remained was, what? He had an idea, but as hard as it was for him to believe he could see ghosts, it was even harder to believe someone else would even think about it.

"Let me tell you what I saw. I saw you walk into that stall, with your eyes going from the horse to the back corner. Back and forth. Then you put a hand on the horse and that was all you did to him. There was nothing said to the animal. No stroking. No patting. I did see you shiver though. The horse did too. That is what I saw. Did I miss anything?"

Father Henry crossed his arms across his black coat and made firm eye contact for the first time. Now William was the one who shifted from side to side and avoided any eye contact. The way he was put on the spot made him uncomfortable, but that was nothing compared to the realization he had reached. It rolled over and over in his head, and his stomach did flips and somersaults as each cycle stopped at the same place, each and every time.

"Father, why don't we head up to the house and talk?"

Neither of the men said anything on the way to the house. Once inside, William motioned to his father's chair at the table. Father Henry's back stayed board straight as his upper body leaned forward and his knees lowered his tall thin frame onto the seat. William held up a glass and a pitcher, to offer some water. It was something he picked up from watching his mother as she welcomed neighbors and friends into their home. With a simple nod, Father Henry accepted, and William poured him a glass of water.

As Father Henry took a sip, William poured himself a glass as well, and gulped it down. His mouth was dry and caked with dust. Which couldn't have been from the work he was doing. The pasture was moist. There wasn't much dust kicked up by either his horse or the plow. Before Father Henry put his glass down on the table, William had already deposited his back in the sink, which he now leaned against, his arms crossed.

Father Henry's glass hit the table and both men looked at one another in dead silence. The only sound William heard was the whooshing of the wind as it raced through one window and out another. It brought a coolness that settled deeper into the corners of the house, where the sunlight couldn't reach. There was a slight shiver moving up William's neck. It wasn't a ghost this time. It was something that frightened him a great deal more. Questions.

"William, why don't you tell me what you saw last night. Did you see her?"

William took a deep swallow to try to soothe his once again parched throat. It didn't help much; his mouth was just as dry. "Her?", he asked. His mind raced. Father Henry saw the girl. How did he?

"Yes, William. I am not a total sensitive, but I have enough in me to know there was a little girl roaming around Gerald's animals. Now, did you feel her, or see her?", Father Henry asked with a blank expression. His tone of voice was very matter of fact. No inflection or waver as he discussed a topic that was not one of normal conversation.

"I saw her," confessed William.

"You did? Is it safe to assume this was not a first?"

William nodded his head.

Father Henry then asked the question that broke William, "How long?"

His body language changed. The upright, arm-crossed man that leaned against the sink became the shoulder-slouched and weak-kneed child that now stumbled for the chair across from Father Henry. There was a great sigh that came from down deep, beyond his physical form, and escaped into the world around them. It was a release. The release of a secret pent up for over a decade. The release of the stress and tension he felt because of his gift. He wasn't alone. There was someone else like him.

7

"I was twelve."

Father Henry removed his black wide-brimmed hat. The fingers of his right hand pinched the top, while the ones on his left traced the brim and made sure everything was straight. Once satisfied, he placed it on the table next to the half-full glass of water. "So, you have been dealing with this for some time now. Let me guess. It starts with a cold shiver on your neck. Maybe a few beads of sweat, and a feeling deep in the pit of your stomach you can't explain. Have I described it so far?"

Upon hearing his gift described so astutely, William straightened his shoulders and sat back in the chair. His wide-open, shocked eyes answered Father Henry's question without uttering a sound, but there was more to add. "I can't explain it, though. It doesn't take me long before I see them."

"William, what do you see? A shadow?"

"Oh, no. Father, I see them. People. I see people, glowing. They disappear and reappear, right in front of me."

The long slender fingers of Father Henry's right hand shot up to his chin and rubbed it as he stared through William. The clarification caught him off guard, and created another nervous silence in the small farmhouse. Among the breeze, William could hear the rough skin of his hand catch on the stubble as it rubbed his chin.

"They look like people to you?"

"Yes, except for the eyes. They are just black and hollow."

This answer was followed by a great deal more rubbing of his chin. William wondered which would wear through first: the stubble, or the skin on his fingers. The chair creaked as he leaned forward, but only at the waist. Father Henry's back remained straight up and down. He mumbled a few phrases to himself. William thought he heard him say, "He is more sensitive than I am," but he wasn't sure he made it out correctly. The mumbling was fast and under his breath.

His next phase was not a mumble, it was a direct question. Its tone more forceful than the previous questions, "Do you talk to them? Interact? You need to tell me."

"Oh, no. They don't respond when I try. I can yell or scream, and they never pay any notice. They only notice when they run into me."

Father Henry's gaze moves from looking through William, to straight into his eyes. There was no blinking in the icy expression, "Run into? You mean they touch you?"

"Yes, Father. Or I touch them. They usually turn or go another way," William answered his question, but grew concerned. This tone and expression was not one he had seen from the normally cheerful priest. The person in front of him had a more foreboding presence.

"And last night?"

"She was walking straight toward the horse, so I stood in between and let her hit me. When she did, she turned and walked through the wall."

"You weren't afraid?"

"I was more concerned with getting kicked by the colt," confessed William.

That answer drew a little chuckle from the grim-faced priest, and gave William the first sight of the person he knew, but it didn't last long. The chuckle and cockeyed smile disappeared. The grim stone-like expression he saw for the previous few moments once again took its place on his face. Deep in thought, his eyes once again stared straight through William. Their gaze was so strong, he could feel it drilling deep into his soul. Powering the drill was a question, a thought, a concern. William knew it. The expression on his guest's face spoke of the gravity of the question.

"William, I need you to be honest with me."

"Of course, Father."

The hands that had stroked the stubble on Father Henry's chin now relaxed to the middle of his chest and faced each other in prayer. "Have you currently, or in the past, practiced the dark arts to summon or invite a spirit, demon, or Lucifer himself into this world?"

The question was a strong right uppercut to William's chin. It knocked him up out of his chair to a stand with an explosion. His quick movements sent the chair teetering behind him before it finally settled down, with all four legs flat on the floor. Father Henry remained stoic; the only movement were his eyes as they followed William up. This was not just a curious friend, or a priest asking about something they'd seen. This was more serious. It was an inquisition, a witch hunt.

There hadn't been one in St. Margaret's Hope in several years, but there had been one in William's lifetime. He remembered it as clear as day. It was a teen girl, Mary SaintClair, if he remembered correctly. She walked around town all hours of the day and night, mumbling to herself. Animals always acted spooked when she neared. Birds seemed to follow her path overhead. Especially the black crows. Flocks upon flocks of crows followed her through town and across the meadows. As the tale goes, Father Henry and several of the town elders went out one night and found her sitting in the middle of an open field with birds all around her. The elders encircled her, and the birds, and walked in slowly and cautiously. As they moved closer to her, the birds cawed like mad before they flew off and left Mary alone in the meadow. She pointed at the elders and mumbled. Several of the elders fell to their knees while the others surrounded her and tied her hands behind her. The next day, a hearing was held. Those that had fallen to their knees testified they'd felt sick to their stomach. Others spoke of how animals had reacted around her, or how the fog parted as she walked through. The hearing was quick, short, and brutal. The sentence was just as quick, short, and brutal. After the verdict was handed down, Mary was taken outside and tied to a stake, where her soul was purged clean by fire. She continued to mumble, not scream, during the purge.

William insisted, "No, Father. This is not something I asked for. They just appear. Honestly, it is nothing more than that."

The stony expression on Father Henry's face cracked. The comforting smile he displayed to his congregation began to show through each of the cracks. Warmth returned to his eyes. Both of which calmed William's nerves. He wasn't sure if what he had said was responsible for this to be honest, he had no proof. He could imagine a similar hearing with John testifying against him, and Gerald adding in what he had seen just last night. The star witness would be Father Henry, who would give a full account of the conversation they'd just had, with a few overdramatic additions for the benefit of the judge, and the spectators.

"William. I understand. Your father was the same way." Father Henry stood up and retrieved his hat from the table. His right hand pinched it at the top, while the left hand traced the brim to make sure it was straight, before he placed it level on his head. On his way to the door he said, "It seems you now have two secrets. I must be going." Without another word or motion toward William, he left out the door. William was left standing in front of a chair with a single thought in his head, *"My father?"*

8

Weeks came and went. The pasture was plowed and planted, and the first sprigs of turnips had broken through the ground. What hadn't broken through were the many questions in William's mind. He had made many trips to town. Some to bring crops to the market. Others for shopping or just coming in for a pint with John.

Many times, he passed Father Henry, but none more frequent than the weekly Sunday holy eucharist. William expected a different look from him, now that he was aware of his secret, but there was nothing. His eyes never settled on him any more than normal when he delivered his sermon from the pulpit. On the way out, he greeted and shook his hand, just like he always had. William debated on whether to approach him himself, maybe that was what he was waiting on, but never did. His gift had made him feel different before, now there was a small side of him that felt that it made him a target, and would rather just blend in with the masses.

It was four weeks after their conversation, William had spent a day out in the field pulling weeds and adding a layer of manure to add some nutrients to the soil. To say he smelled like shit was an understatement. Even the animals moved away from him as he passed on his way to the farmhouse. A bath was in order, but it would take days to get the smell out of his hands. When he opened the door to the farmhouse, he was surprised to find two guests sitting at his table. Both of the guest were surprised by the stench that came through the door with William.

Neither guest recoiled with a repulsed look on their face. Just a little twitch of their nose, and a wider than normal opening of their eyes, were the only visible signs from the two proper men seated at the table. Each had already made themselves at home. Both with a glass of water on the table, one a little emptier than the other. Two black wide-brimmed hats sat on the table next to each glass. The men sat upright, their focus was fixed on William, who stood in the doorway, more than a bit startled by the scene in his house.

"Father?" William asked, in an attempt to seem cordial and less alarmed. Inside, his mind screamed, *"What are you doing in my house?"*

"Excuse the intrusion, William. There is someone I need you to meet. Please come in and have a seat."

William held both his hands up to remind Father Henry of his current unclean state. The saying is cleanliness is next to godliness, and there was a whole lot of godliness in the room for him to be that unclean. "Do you mind if I clean up while we talk?"

"Of course not."

William stood over the sink and used a large block of soap to lather up his hands and arms. The fat-based soap produced a nice layer of brown up to his elbow. Father Henry started to talk as William poured water out of the pitcher to rinse his arms for the first time. Based on his best guess, he would have maybe three more rinses before he would need to pump more water.

"William, this is Bishop Emmanuel. He has come a long way to meet you. He is interested in your gift."

The distinguished white-haired gentleman seated to Father Henry's left stood up. He was quite a bit shorter than both Father Henry and William. He almost gave the appearance of being frail, but when he extended his hand to William, the scars and callouses from a hard life were obvious. Instead of meeting his hand, William held up two still-stained soap and filth caked hands. The bishop withdrew his hand and looked around the room, while uttering, "Excuse`"

The word meant nothing to William, but the accent he heard meant everything. He was not from around here, not even close. It was one he had never heard before. The only way he could describe it was smooth, and pleasant to the ears. The look he gave Father Henry conveyed the question he had in his head.

"That's right, William. He is Italian."

He would have to trust Father Henry on that. There was no other option. William had never met an Italian. It would only be an assumption that he was from Italy, a place he had only heard about and seen on a map in school. That was one of those far off places that was out there. Out in the rest of the world that William had dreamed of visiting to find his greater purpose, his adventure. Now, someone from one of those far-off places stood in front of him, in his farmhouse.

"Vatican City, to be more precise," continued Father Henry.

That fact astonished William more than the first. He knew where and what the Vatican City was. He also knew what that meant, but that couldn't be. Father Murray was Anglican, a prince of the Church of England, not exactly a favored bedfellow of the Vatican. If you said they were mortal enemies, that might be considered a stretch for some, but considering the wars and lives lost, others might consider it true. The Vatican and its princes were forced out of England and the dutchy of Scotland, by King Henry the VIII because of a difference in principles. Even this long after that schism, it was still considered a crime against the crown to associate with anyone from the Vatican. William knew that, and he assumed Father Henry knew that. How could he not?

William ignored the shock and alarm that ran through his bones. His imagination had the king's guards standing outside his door, just waiting to break it down. After a swallow to clear his throat, and to push his imagination out of the way, he managed to say, "It's nice to meet you Bishop Emmanuel."

"The pleasure is mine, William," said the scratchy Italian voice. He continued, " Father Henry tells me you can see ghosts and interact with them."

"Yes, I see them. I can't talk to them."

Emmanuel looked back at Father Henry, who explained William's response. "No, he can't talk to them, but he can touch them... or... I guess the better way to say it is, they are aware of him when they come in contact with him, and move away."

Emmanuel turned back to William, and studied him, up and down. "Oh, I see. What do you feel?"

William clarified, "You mean, when they walk through me?"

The bishop merely dipped his head forward.

"Cold. Very Cold. Wherever they touch is cold as they pass through."

The two visitors shared a common inquisitive look at each other. William may have had the same look on his face. Questions filled his mind at the moment, and so far, no answers had been offered.

"William, why don't you have a seat?", Father Henry requested. Bishop Emmanuel returned to his seat; hands folded on his lap. Both men watched him as he sat, spots of unrinsed soap clung to his arms. When his weight settled on the chair, he sat and looked back and forth at both men for what was next. The problem was, neither of them verbalized a response. Instead, they once again shared inquisitive looks at each other. It was as if this was their own secret language. *"Maybe it was something they were taught at seminary school,"* thought William.

"William, you have a gift," explained Bishop Emmanuel. "One that very few have. Those that do, are called *sensitivo*. As you can imagine, everyone is not the same. Some people can feel their presence. Some are stronger than others. They can... read their... I mean, hear their thoughts. It is strong enough in others to catch a glimpse of them as they move in and out of our world. Some see them, but then there are the ones like you; the rarest of all. Those that can see them, and touch or talk to them. It is a very special gift bestowed upon your family by God, to have that ability."

"To put it in some perspective William, Emmanuel explained to me earlier that there are less than what... a dozen families with your ability?" Father Henry looked at his fellow visitor for confirmation, which he received with an astute and thoughtful nod.

He knew he was different, and had only ever heard Father Henry describe it as a gift. What was a gift for one person, could be considered a curse to others. To William, he also considered it more of the latter. It was something he hid from everyone; he hadn't even talked to his father about it. John was the only confidante he told, and that was because he was there once, and that was all. If he hadn't been there that one time, he would have never said anything. The same with Father Henry. There was something else, though. Another phrase that had been repeated again, for the second time. This phrase was stuck in his craw, but was surging up and forward until it exploded out of William's mouth, "You said this was given to my family. What about my family?"

"It is like a royal bloodline. Your bloodline has this ability," answered Bishop Emmanuel.

"William, I don't know for sure, but I do recall several conversations with your father about him feeling an evil wind, or something not of this world, out there," interjected Father Henry. He continued, with a hint of a warning in his voice, "Now, I could be reading something into his statements that was not real, but knowing about you, now..." His face crinkled to make a flat smile.

William knew what he meant. It was a logical leap. What struck him, though, there was nothing William could recall that would lead him to believe his father could see ghosts. He was always a strong willed and confident man, who spoke his mind. That had even cost him some friends over the years. A strong lesson his father had once taught him, not everyone really wants to hear the truth. He would just have to accept that the truth might hurt some. William and John saw plenty examples of that during the verbal fights their fathers would engage in. It always started the same way; William's father would state a truth that John's father wasn't ready to hear. They always ended the same way too. John's father walking away, convinced he had won the argument. William and his father walking away as his father stated, "He just wasn't ready for the truth". Each of them may have been covered in mud or dirt, if the argument was tense enough.

Through all those truths and speaking of his mind, William couldn't remember once where his father had hinted at this gift. Not anything that matched the comments Father Henry mentioned. It was possible that such things were not stated in mixed company. That was all in the past now, the question that sat in front of William now was, what's next? He found it hard to accept that someone came all the way from the Vatican, with the travel and the risk, just to sit in his kitchen and tell him about something he pretty much already knew.

"Well, my father never said anything about it to me, if he did have what you call is 'the gift'. Gentleman, what can I do for you?" William looked at Bishop Emmanuel. His eyes bristled with all the confidence he could muster up, "I am sure you didn't come all this way to tell me what I already knew."

Both gentlemen seem surprised, and relieved, by William's newfound confidence. It didn't shock or take them aback. If anything, it drew smiles from the two men. Father Henry's was one of pleasure and approval. William had to assume the Bishop's was the same, but it was hard to tell. It looked painful to move the weathered and wrinkled skin on his face enough to produce an expression that pushed the cheeks up on his gaunt face.

They were locked in their secret language once again, exchanging looks and an occasional mumble with one another. The uncomfortable feelings William had, were now growing into frustration. Was there a point to all this, or could it really be he was just there to explain to William about his gift? Maybe the Bishop was the first of many visitors that will show up at his door. He was now Father Henry's religious sideshow act for those in the clergy. *"Come with me and meet a man that sees ghosts,"* William could imagine him barking at a crowd of monks and priests. *"Only one of his kind in the emerald isle, come see him now!"*, would be another line. If that was it, he had picked the wrong attraction. William had more important tasks to tend to than to be a storyteller, or asked over and over if he could see a ghost in the room with them.

"Gentlemen, I am here. What is this all about? It's been a long day and I need to finish cleaning up." The stench that still hung in the room anchored his last point.

Neither man seemed flummoxed by the interruption. If anything, they appeared to understand and finished their conclave together by deciding who would talk next

"William, as we stated, you are rare. You are also valuable. Your skills are needed by the Church, to serve a greater good... a greater purpose. Bishop Emmanuel is here to offer you an opportunity to fulfill that purpose."

There was a good chance Father Henry was playing the strings inside William's heart, and he knew it. Those strings were laid out in front of him during the many conversations Father Henry and William had during his childhood, about his longing for something greater. Now was he strumming them like a minstrel, or was *this* that longing William had felt? That 'something' in his bloodline, as both men had stated, knew there was something more. That 'something' asked, "What is the opportunity?"

Bishop Emmanuel explained, "There is much more you can do with your gift, but it requires training. Training the Church is willing to provide in return for service."

"Service, you mean in the conscripts?"

"In a way, yes," Father Henry said. "Not in the military mind you. There are spots around the world that are more spiritual than others. Ghosts, or spirits," he corrected, " tend to gather in those locations. For hundreds of years, the Church has assigned those like you to be their caretaker. To tend to both the living and the dead. If you accept, you will travel to the Vatican and be trained on how to handle the spirits you encounter. At the end of your training, you will be assigned a location. William, will you accept?"

Father Henry and Bishop Emmanuel leaned forward in their chairs toward William. Both looked at him with anticipation. William wasn't sure what to say. This was his ticket to leave and see the world beyond the ocean. It could also be that greater calling he felt pull at his soul for as long as he could remember. There was no way to know without trying. If he accepted though, it meant he would leave all he has known behind, which included the farm that had been in his family for centuries. That was not a trivial thing to William. He could almost hear his descendants rolling over beneath their gravestones.

"Can I have some time to think it over?", William asked.

"I leave in four days. If you accept, you will need to return with me then."

William said, "I understand," as he sat back in his chair. He did. He understood everything, but he still didn't have a clue what his decision would be.

9

To say the question weighed on William would be an understatement. No matter what he was doing, or where he was, it was there. Whether working his crops, caring for his livestock, walking through the meadow to clear his head, or even in the outhouse trying to clear something else, the question remained clouding any other thought passing through his mind. It was always there in the front of his mind.

With two days left before Bishop Emmanuel was scheduled to depart, William made a special trip into town and sat on his rock. It was unusually clear that afternoon. The normal marine layer wasn't there. Instead of a horde of fluffy white clouds passing above the horizon line, there was a majestic blue, just a few shades lighter than the dark blue ocean below it. He needed his rock. Really, he needed the clarity he felt while sitting there and pondering, several times in the past. It was while he sat on that very rock, several years ago, that he told Ainslee how he felt. It was also there where he decided they would need to keep their feelings private. Both decisions helped him quiet a yearning, and the voices of doubt that came with it. He needed that now.

Having no clue which way Italy was, William guessed and faced that direction. It was silly, he knew. At that distance he would see nothing but the ocean. That is all he ever saw from that perch, no matter which direction he looked, but this time was different. This time he had an opportunity to go beyond the horizon and see what was out there. Maybe it was that opportunity that clouded his thoughts the most. If he turned it down now, would he ever have another opportunity? It was doubtful. Visitors didn't pass through this way often, and none with such an offer.

As good as the offer seemed, there was a great bit of fear that went with it. William still didn't know what he would really be asked to do. All Father Henry and Bishop Emmanuel had said was, he would be the caretaker for a place. They hadn't provided any description of what a caretaker did, but they had talked about training. What was there to train on? He already knew how to see and stand in front of ghosts. That was his best natural talent, no one needed to teach him how to do that. The humorous thought that maybe they wanted him to teach them crossed his mind. He pictured himself standing in front of a great hall somewhere, in a grand robe, probably red or blue, with a hat. A hundred sets of eyes focused on him as he lectured them on the art of ghost seeing. He almost chucked out loud at the thought of his lecture, *"And this is how you do it. If you see a ghost, you step in front of it. That is all there is to it."*

The humor brought a smile to his face and helped to push back the fear for a moment, but another problem was behind him, literally behind him. Everything he knew, from the day he was born to this moment, was behind him in this town. His friends, his family's farm, and Ainslee. That last one pulled at his heart a tad more than the others. The thought of never laying his eyes on her again sent a bolt of cold through his core. Not the usual warmth he felt when he thought of her, or heard her voice. A warmth that, to him, felt like the morning sun and could clear any fog or feeling of cold depression away from his soul. A warmth that now spread from his left ear across his face, as the voice of an angel, his angel, whispered, "What are you doing?"

William didn't turn toward her as she joined him on his rock. She tried a few times to have him rename it their rock, but that was a point he wouldn't yield. It was his, he saw it first, he sat on it first. In his mind, both of those defined ownership. Together, they sat on his rock. She leaned ever so slightly against him, with her right arm locked around his left, at the elbow.

"Thinking?" she asked.

"Yes," William replied, with a sigh. His gaze was still locked on the horizon in front of them.

"What about?"

He knew she would ask. She always did. Of course, this time the answer wouldn't be the normal, *"Wondering what is out there"* response. William wasn't even sure he could tell her the truth. Well, he knew he couldn't tell her the whole truth, that was for sure. "Things. I might be going on a trip for a bit."

He felt her whole body turn toward him in response. A sharpening of her breath accompanied the wide-open stare of her beautiful green eyes.

"Father Henry has a visitor from...," William almost slipped up. Ainslee's family was still royalty. He couldn't take the chance that she wouldn't tell her father, and he would feel some old loyalty to the crown. "From the mainland. He offered to take me back with him, to show me what is out there." William felt that was a plausible excuse. He knew she was aware of how strong his desire to see the outside world was. Hell, she even shared it. There was no doubt in his mind, while she might be hurt, she would understand it.

"Just like that. You are going to up and leave?", she asked.

"Yes."

His terse reply was met with several more short and sharp breaths. Was it possible? Did he have miss prim and proper in a huff? She swiveled next to him like a sign blowing in the breeze. First, she looked at him, and then back out into the ocean, then back at him, and then the ocean. This continued several more times until she stopped and faced away from him.

"It's my chance. To get out of here, you know?" Before William could finish, she asked a question, hushed, under her breath. This was no attempt to hide the question from anyone passing by. His announcement had stripped the will out of her voice as she asked. "What about me?"

"We have been through all this. Your father would never..."

"Goddamnit, William Miller," anger had replaced the will in her voice. "Stop using my father as an excuse. You have no reason to hide from him."

William peered to his side. Her eyes were fixed and watering, but fire burned in her cheeks. She had a temper; he had seen it before, in their youth. In truth, he had seen it more than once. Her reactions to some poor joke or prank he and John had pulled while on the cusp of adolescence. Girls tend to mature before boys, add in a touch of nobility and proper upbringing, and that gap increases. If you asked Ainslee, John and William had yet to grow up. This was different than those times, though. This was no stupid joke or prank. He wouldn't be letting her off the hook anytime soon to laugh while she calmed down. Her next move told him there would be no calming down.

The always outspoken, never lost for words, Ainslee McLayer stood up and walked off into the sunset. Her hair flowed in the wind as her shape was silhouetted by the setting sun. William wanted to call out to her, but couldn't muster either the voice, or the words to say. There was nothing to say except goodbye, and he hated those. No one ever left St. Margaret's Hope, unless they died. This goodbye pained him deeper than any of the deaths he could remember. Perhaps it was easier this way.

10

The night began with sleep forgetting to pay William a visit. He laid in his bed and waited, but it never arrived. Perhaps it waited for his mind and heart to join the rest of his body beneath the covers. Those were still perched on the rock that overlooked the harbor. He sat there for another hour, and waited and hoped for Ainslee to return, but when the sun dipped below the buildings, darkness was cast on his body and his hopes. As he walked away, he stopped to look back a few times, to check and see if she had come back. He knew the chance was slim, but even the slimmest of hopes was hope enough.

"This is how it had to be, " was the phrase he repeated to himself. It sounded good, and made sense, at least that is what he told himself. He wasn't sure how much he was buying that argument. What was it his father had told him that time he had gotten caught in a briar patch? *The slower he moved, the longer it would hurt, just run quick. It would hurt, but it would be over soon.* Maybe this was like that. Cutting all personal ties, quickly and completely, would make it easier to leave. No connections. Nothing to hold him back. That thought caused the heart that had just rejoined the rest of his exhausted and emotional body in bed to sink. Sleep followed the darkness he felt.

The rest wasn't long, though. Warmth radiated over William from across the room, like a raging fire. Half asleep, William thought he had left a fire burning in the fireplace. Something his father had warned him about many times. It was ok to leave the embers in the fire to supply warmth during the worst of the winter, but careless to leave anything more. A rogue ember floating in the hot air as it rose up in the house, or a shift in the stack sending an engulfed log rolling out into the room, could be all it took to burn down the farmhouse.

William pushed off his blanket to allow more of the night air to cool his body, but relief was not what he found. The source of the heat took aim at his exposed arms and legs, and began to cook them to the point of being uncomfortable, even painful. He rolled over and cracked a single eye open to check the fireplace. The fire he saw was not in the fireplace, it encompassed a shirtless man seated at his table. It had the head of a goat, with a crown made of a dried vine with large thorns pointing out from all sides. A dark brown blood oozed down its head where the thorns pierced through the fur-covered skull. Snorts of smoke accompanied every breath. The yellow centers of its red eyes peeled away at the layers of William's soul.

He blinked several times to clear what had to be a leftover nightmare that was stuck in his consciousness somewhere between asleep and awake, but each blink revealed the same creature seated there. Now both eyes were open and looked straight at the beast. His breath raced along with his pulse. Deep inside, a little voice yelled "run" as loud as it could, but the fear he felt washed the voice away. The sensation was new. William didn't fear much. Something he credited to what Father Henry and Bishop Emmanuel called his gift. Once you are used to seeing ghosts, not much else could frighten you, but this was not a ghost.

"I see you there, looking at me. I am real. Not a dream," it said in a thundering, coarse voice, that was half man and half animal.

William said nothing. He couldn't. The lump of grey matter between his ears struggled with the appearance of his visitor. Verbalizing a logical coherent thought out loud was way too much to ask. Sitting up and swinging his legs out of the bed was all he could muster.

"Don't get up. I won't stay." The creature put both hands flat on the table and pushed himself up. The flames rose high against the ceiling. William watched the path of the flames as the beast moved around the table. To his surprise, nothing caught fire as the flames passed over them, but the heat grew in intensity as it moved closer, as did the glare of the yellow-centered eyes. It leaned back against the table and crossed its cloven-hoofed feet, one over the other.

"Speaking of staying, " it continued, "you really should stay here. You have a great home, a sweet lassie, and a great crop this year and every year for the rest of your life. The envy of every farmer around, that is what you will be. Especially when you and Ainslee have those two large strapping boys to help out around here." It looked in the direction of one of the windows and said, "By the looks of it, you need to start on those boys soon, you are going to need lots of help. I have never seen a crop so full. Why don't you have a look?" It then extended its left arm and pointed with its skinny, bony finger. A line of flame shot from it and pushed the window open.

William's body didn't move. His eyes looked in that direction as far as he could, but his ass, and the rest of him, remained one with the bed. All he could see from there was the dark night sky outside, and the roofline of his slaughterhouse.

It extended its other hand toward him, and one by one curled all five fingers back into its palm. When the final finger reached the palm, William felt his feet leave the floor and his ass leave the bed. He floated first toward the creature, but before he reached it, he turned toward the window, where he was placed down on his feet. Now he had a perfect view of a clear night, with a full moon that was not expected for another ten days. The light of the unscheduled Corn Moon illuminated his pasture, the pasture he had weeded and spread manure in just days before. A pasture that was now full of lush green tops of turnips. A sight that was both too early, and too good, to be true. William had never seen a crop that good before, not on his farm, or anyone else's, to be honest.

From behind him the voice growled, "You have no reason to leave." The phrase echoed over and over as four people walked through the crops. He recognized Ainslee and himself, joined at the hand, walking. On either side them were two young men. Both were bigger than him. Everyone was laughing and smiling. They stopped to wave at the window, and then continued on their stroll.

William woke up the next morning to the sound of a rooster welcoming the dawn of a new day, a cold one at that. Even under two blankets, the chill shook his bones as he stirred awake. The remnants of a dream from his slumber hung over him. Before he opened his eyes, he turned his head toward the center of the room. Then, with one eye, and only one eye, he peeked. There was nothing there, which relieved him as well as helped to settle the question in his mind. *Was this real or just a dream?*

William swung both legs out of the bed and reached for his shirt. A stretch preceded a walk across the room to start a small fire to knock off the chill and prepare his breakfast. Two eggs sounded good to him, and a hot cup of coffee would warm him right up. The nightshirt he wore to sleep in was deposited over the chair as he put on one he had washed several days ago. He walked over and shut the window and headed across to fetch his pot for coffee, but stopped as he passed the table. There, as clear as day, were two handprints burnt into the surface.

11

William couldn't shake the events of the previous night. No matter how hard he worked in the field, it didn't distract his mind from two questions. Was it real or a dream? If it was real, what the hell was it? Neither question had an answer that came right away. Instead, it was a circular spiral. There was no way that was real, but what about the handprints? A few minutes later he would repeat the same circle. The only thought that broke the cycle from time to time was the reminder that he saw ghosts. Could it be that hard to believe he saw such a vision?

If that was true, this was no ordinary ghost. That left only one possibility, it was a demon. If that were true, it would be the first he had seen. The next question would be why? It had shown him the images of a good life, but said that would be possible if he stayed. Was he trying to keep him from leaving? If so, there was that same question again, why? Why would a demon care?

The logical side of his mind submitted another argument for consideration. This was all a figment of his imagination caused by the stress he felt over the decision to leave his farm, Ainslee, and everything he knew, behind. To him that made sense, and when he thought about the handprints, he remembered how dirty he was the day Father Henry and Bishop Emanuel had come to visit. He had sat in that exact spot, perhaps he put his hands down there.

At the end of the day, William was more mentally exhausted than physically. Tomorrow was the day. The day he would walk away and start a new adventure. He had one last task to tend to, though. He had to tell John. His friend of all of his life was sure to have questions, and not just a few. William hoped giving him his farm would be more than enough to distract him and stop some of the questions.

While the sun still peeked above the rise of the hills in the distance, William made the walk over to John's. He knocked on his door and called his name, as he always did. An act that annoyed John's wife, Mary, more often than not, especially at this time of night when she puts down their two young boys. Luckily for her, this was the last time.

He waited outside for John, who emerged from the door before William called out for him again. John came out, as he always did, hands motioning for him to keep it down, which was, in most cases, too late. The children would be awake by the second or third call. No such interruption tonight, William had only called out once, and then backed away to wait. John walked toward him and asked, "Is everything ok, William? Is there something wrong?"

William stood and fidgeted with a rock that was under his foot. On the way over he rehearsed the talk a few times, and a few ways. The way he decided to start was not any of those. Instead, he took a page from how he had told Ainslee the day before. "I am leaving tomorrow," he said.

"Leaving?", John asked. His face and posture shocked straight.

"Yes. You know how long I have wondered what else is out there. I have a chance to find out." William talked while he looked down and fidgeted with the same rock.

"Okay," John said. His tone asked a dozen questions. The expression on his face asked a dozen more. "Where are you going, and when?"

"Tomorrow. I don't know where." The rock was getting a good working on. The dirt under it had been depressed and anything loose had rolled out of the way by the constant back and forth motion caused by William's foot.

"Tomorrow?", John exclaimed. William looked up at him and then toward his door. He half expected to see Mary walk out with that look on her face.

In a calmer voice, William said, "Yep, tomorrow. The farm's yours. The crops are planted. My sow has another two or three months to go. The chickens have eggs every morning, just make sure you check them, and you already know about the cow." John's own cow became sick a few months ago and started to produce foul milk. After he put her down, William and John shared William's cow. Each took turns milking and caring for her.

William had said what he needed to say, then he added, "You have been a great friend, John," and then held out his hand. John took it, but William could tell it was more of a reaction than a willful movement. After a quick shake, William turned and walked back in the direction of his farmhouse. John stood there, hand still held out, and watched his friend of forever walk away. Before William reached the stone wall that separated the two tracks of land, John sprinted after him.

"William!", he called. The huff and puff of heavy breathing emphasized every syllable of his name. This was probably the fastest John had run since they were teenagers. William stopped, but didn't turn toward John.

When John reached him, he asked, "What is this all about?"

"It is exactly what I said."

"So, you are going to leave, just as simple as that?"

"Yes, simple as that." William didn't mince words. There was no point to. Nothing John could say would change his mind, and he didn't want to give him the chance. He said, "'Night, John. Take care," and started toward his house. He wasn't good with farewells, especially those where the person was still living.

Inside, he turned in a little earlier than usual. He intended to get up early and head straight to town to meet Father Henry and Bishop Emmanuel before dawn, to tell them his decision. For the second night, sleep failed to arrive when needed. For the second night, he felt a hole in the pit of his soul. All the memories, his childhood, the life he knew, were left out there at the break in the fence where he had walked away from John. He tried to focus on what was ahead of him, but the past always crept in. Memories of summer afternoons in the fields with John. The times they'd snuck a little of his father's whiskey out to the wall. Moments of mischief they'd got each other into, and the moments of heartache they'd both experienced with the loss of their parents, and then there was Ainslee. Vision after vision of her walking with them. The sun highlighting her auburn hair. She was the last vision he saw, as his mind gave in to the exhaustion and despair he felt. Familiar old creaks and shudders of his home were the last sounds he heard before his world descended into black.

For the second time in consecutive nights, sleep didn't last long. This time there wasn't an unbearable heat baking him in his bed, nor was there a blast of cold air chilling his bones. Instead, the room was comfortable. Embers continued to glow orange in the hearth, to produce warm air that circulated around the room. What was there was a presence. A presence behind him. One that watched him, and it was close. After what was there, or not, last night, there was no desire to turn over fast. So, he rolled his head as far as he could, with the hope of getting a glimpse out of the corner of his eye at whatever it was. All he saw was his ceiling, so he let his body shift ever so slightly to bring it into view.

Instead of a creature of flame with a goat head, there was the shape of a beautiful woman with long hair. She stood just a few feet from his bed, with her hands held together in front of her. In the darkness he couldn't see her face, but could tell she had soft features. A sense of calm tranquility filled the room, along with the scents of lavender and lilac.

12

"William Miller. Do you really think you can just walk out on me like that?" The voice, one William considers the one of an angel in normal situations, had a tad of vinegar and a heavy dose of perturbation in it.

"Ainslee, how did you get in here?", William asked as he sat up half-asleep, and rubbed his eyes. He scooted over to give her a spot to sit on the bed, but she had no intention of sitting. What William thought were hands crossed in front of her, was her hands on her hips. Her left foot tapped at a furious level, and thanks to the small ambient light the embers created, he saw she was biting her lip. Seeing that was a warning to him. Running off in a huff yesterday was just the first stage of her temper. The biting of the lip was stage four, and preceded the final explosion. The other two stages, pacing, and blowing the hair out of her face over and over again, must have taken place at her home throughout the day.

"I am waiting, Will." She ignored his question, and didn't change her stance.

"Yes, now I need some sleep. You need to get home before your father, or someone notices you are gone." William braced for the impact that he knew was brewing underneath. That was when he saw something new, another blow of her hair out of her face followed by a hair flip to remove the strands that fell from a slight, but constant, bob of her head. This was serious. If there had been more light, he was sure he would see her cheeks flushed red.

"Don't you dare try to tell me what to do, and enough about my father." The foot still tapped as she resumed biting her bottom lip. "But I will tell YOU what to do."

She paused and William got up and slipped on his boots and shirt. There didn't appear to be any hope she would leave on her own. Even if she did, he wouldn't feel right if she walked back on her own. The shirt slid over his head and he went to put an arm around her. "Let's walk you home..." he started to say, but she ducked his arm and retreated to the other side of the room. Now her arms were crossed in front of her. The bottom lip was still getting worked on.

"No. I am not going anywhere. You are going to take me with you." The statement that escaped her mouth caught them both by surprise. Ainslee was the most surprised of all, her hand shot up to cover her mouth, as if to stop the words. The biting of the lip and foot tapping stopped, and pacing began.

"Come on, let me walk you home."

She held up a single finger as she paced back and forth deep, in thought. Her left hand was on her hip, the right one soon joined it. This was different than how he had found her when he woke up. Then she was angry, now her shoulders were loose, and the wheels in her head were hard at work. Arguments and counter arguments that took place in her eyes, were mouthed by her lips. She froze, and said, "Yes, that is it. Take me with you."

"No, that is not it. Let me walk you home," insisted William.

"Why not? We have talked for years about wanting to know what else is out there. Why should you be the only one to find out?"

"This is nonsense, Ainslee. I have a big day tomorrow and need to get some sleep. Let's get you home."

There was no give in her. She stood her ground firmly. "No. It's settled. Take me with you. It actually solves two problems."

She was a woman who, once her mind was made up, there was no changing it, even when she was wrong. That was a trait that William normally found humorous and charming, but not now. He was in no mood to go around and around with her, as they had many times before, and needed to put this to a stop. "You are being silly, let's go." William knew as soon as he said it, he hadn't put an end to it, not even close. He knew the trap of calling one of her notions "silly" and he had walked right into it.

"You don't want to hear what it will solve?"

"Sure," he said. Knowing this would take a bit, and there would be no stopping her until she was finished, William walked to the table and had a seat. He reached forward into his stack of sulfur matches and flicked it on his flint stone. There was a quick spark before a small yellow flame appeared on the end. Before it went out, William pushed it into his oil lamp and lit the wick, sending flickers of light through the room. Two turns of the wheel splashed bright light across the entire room. The vision in front of him caused his heart to skip a beat. Ainslee stood there in a blue dress, with hair fixed as if she were headed to Sunday mass. The vision was one that forced his head to question his decision to leave all over again.

"Well, first," she started her pacing again, as if she were about to give a lecture in a great hall. "We both want to leave St. Margaret's Hope. It is something we have talked about since we were young. This is a point you cannot disagree with."

William resisted a roll of his eyes at her use of the full word, "cannot".

"Opportunities like this don't come around often. If either of us turn it down, there may not be another chance."

"Well, first, the offer was not made to..." William attempted to reply to her argument for point one, but she shushed him and held up a hand while she continued to pace. "No response, until I have said both points, please." He had to resist a second urge to roll his eyes.

"Second, you refuse to talk to my father and ask for my hand. "

"Now, wait a moment." That point hit William right between the eyes, and stung at that. He stood up, but she stopped his attempt to respond further.

"Uh. Uh. Uh... let me finish."

Finish, he would let her, but listen to this anymore he would not. The decision was made, and this was just a waste of time for William. It did cross his mind that this may make things easier on her, but it made it worse on him.

Ainslee continued, "As I said, you won't talk to my father. So, we leave and go live our own life and you won't have to." She paused for a moment. William thought he saw her swallow hard and the emergence of a single tear on her cheek. Another hard swallow, followed by two loud sighs, ended the pacing. She turned toward him, a second tear on the other cheek. Her look less determined, and more of a plea, with a slight pout in her lips. What fire had been there earlier was gone, in fact her cheeks looked pale, more than just her normal fair complexion. The color had been drained from them as she turned toward him. A slight shake appeared in her body. The shake progressed to a tremble.

"Ainslee, are you ok?" William got up and moved around the table to her. Taking her by the arm, he helped her to a chair at the table, where he sat her down. When he tried to release her arm, her hands reached up and grabbed his, and wouldn't let go. They felt warm to him, but the expression on her colorless face looked cold and scared. She pulled his hands closer to her cheek. The skin felt soft and cool against his hard rough hands. Her big eyes looked up and her pink lips uttered a two word phrase toward him, her voice pleading with each syllable.

"Marry me."

"What?", asked William.

Gripping his hands tighter, as if to never let go, she pleaded, "You heard me. Let's start this life together, as husband and wife. You don't even have to talk to my father. I know you have wanted to forever, you're just too afraid to ask my father. You don't have to now. You don't. It is just us. You told me you are leaving with someone here visiting Father Henry. We could have him marry us before we left. I know he would do it, and he wouldn't tell anyone. William, this is our chance. I can't let you leave. We are meant to be together. Marry me. Marry me right now."

William stood there in stunned silence, mind swimming with what she had said. He looked down at her. She looked up at him. "Okay."

13

In the middle of the night, mixed among the normal creaks and groans of Father Henry's modest timber raftered residence, was a single rhythmic rap. The nightly drop in temperatures and coastal breeze gave the single room building a voice all its own, but this new knock was not part of this voice. Every so often, what sounded like a loud tap paused before it started again. This pattern continued for several minutes before a new sound was added to the chorus of creaks, groans, and taps.

"Father Henry?", whispered a voice through the brown-stained planks of his door.

The tapping resumed before a hint of light showed through the gaps in the door. Two large clunks were heard on the other side before the door cracked open. A single candle, held by the priest's elderly hand, threw shadows on his face from below. Still half asleep and in his white sleep shirt, his weary eyes peered out at William.

"Son, everything alright?"

"Yes, Father. Well, kind of..." William moved a step to the side to expose Ainslee McLayer behind him.

Father Henry did everything but jump in surprise at the sight of her there at that ungodly hour of night. The door flung inward as he motioned with his right hand to usher them inside in a hurry. When both had entered, Father Henry stuck his head outside and looked around for anyone else, or anyone that might see these two young members of his flock coming inside. Inside there was a simple wooden table, with four chairs, in the center of the room. Along the stacked stone walls sat an assortment of furniture. A single table with a wash basin sat in the corner. A tin pitcher sat on top of the table. In the opposite corner was a writing desk. The surface sloped down, but a single ledge kept a stack of papers from sliding off; an inkwell and pen sat on the flat top. Two simple bunk-style beds were pushed up against the wall, the tossed covers in one showed which bed Father Henry had emerged from. The other's occupant still slept inside. A few snorts and snores emerged.

Over the next hour, William and Ainslee sat at the table and, in hushed tones, explained their plan to the priest. Father Henry made several modest appeals to change their minds. Each time, Ainslee was able to present a counterargument. William never tried, or never had the opportunity to, before she jumped in when Father Henry took a breath. When he was finally satisfied, they had thought this through, he leaned back in his chair, crossed his arms over his chest, and stared at the flame dancing on the tall candle in the center of the table. Or that was what the two believed he was focused on. On the table in front of the candle was a simple black leather-bound book. Several ribbons, of various colors, protruded out, marking pages of significance. On the cover, a single gold cross. Father Henry hoped for divine guidance from the good book.

He looked up at the two who sat across from him, both looked on with rapt attention and leaned closer to the table. "This changes things, then." He pushed back from the table, and sat there for a second, lost in thought. He then stood up and said, "Wait here."

Father Henry went over and roused Bishop Emmanuel, who woke up just as disoriented as his counterpart had before he opened the door. William could see Father Henry motion in their direction, which drew an inquisitive look from the bishop. This spawned a hushed conversation between the two. A shake of the bishop's head here, another there, and several exaggerated hand motions, told William the discussion was not going well. He tried to hear what was said, but they talked too quietly, and the light was too low to allow him to see their lips. If he had to guess at the objections the bishop would be making, the rushed wedding would be top on the list. The church viewed the union between man and woman to be one of the most sacred. Anyone rushing into it was counseled against it. That was probably the conversation they were having now. How William would deal with this objection, he didn't know. He hoped the bishop would listen to their reasons.

Father Henry left the side of his compatriot, and walked back toward the table. The flat smile on his face dripped with concern. Behind him, the bishop got out of bed and headed to a wash basin, mumbling the whole way. William prepared himself to hear that the bishop objected. As he grabbed Ainslee's hand, he hoped she had the same thoughts he had had, and prepared herself too. Instead of coming directly to the table, Father Henry made a stop at a simple dressing table with a single drawer. It rattled back and forth on the wood runners as he pulled it open. After a quick search he pulled out a single piece of lace and then searched again. What he emerged with, William couldn't see. It was a small object that he held in his closed hand.

Back at the table, Father Henry laid the lace out flat on the table and used his hand to smooth out a few bumps and wrinkles. He took great care with this task. A tug here, and a tug there to straighten it, his right hand clenched into a tight fist all the while. The lace was then folded in half, and then half again, to produce a square of white lace. A square that Father Henry pulled along the table to center straight in front of him. The straight smile across his face bent upward. The fourth, and last, chair at the table slid out. Bishop Emmanuel sat, still drying his face with a towel, he seemed neither refreshed nor awake.

William prepared himself for a lecture, but it never arrived. Instead, Father Henry opened his hand to reveal two rings. He placed both on the square of lace, as if to display them. William believed he had seen these rings before, but wasn't sure where. Father Henry wore several during his services, but he assumed those were ones embossed with the crest of the Church of England. A scan of his hands, and those of the bishop, revealed they both wore several rings on both hands. Each of the rings were similar, but different. That made sense to William, since their own church and its traditions were rooted in Catholicism, much of which is the same, just with different symbols and terms.

"Bishop Emmanuel has agreed to take both of you with him, but this does complicate things. Far more than you can understand. First things first, though, let's get you two married. You will need to leave before daybreak to avoid being seen." With his look and the tone of his voice, it was obvious the last statement was meant for Ainslee. "These rings are ones I have held on to for a dear friend for several years. William, that was your father. These are your father and mother's rings. On his deathbed he asked me to hold them until you were older, and ready. I see no reason why that time is not now. With this piece of lace, we will join your hands together in union."

"A union that cannot be broken," added Bishop Emmanuel, with the hint of a wry smile.

Father Henry continued with a chuckle, "Yes, one that cannot be broken. Bishop Emmanuel will perform the ceremony. I will be the witness. I assume you both understand what that means?"

Both William and Ainslee looked at each other. With smiles plastered across both of their faces, they nodded. They would now be wed in the eyes of the Catholic Church, and have to abide by the rules therein. That wasn't a problem for William, he couldn't ever imagine a scenario where he would want to leave. He hoped she felt the same.

The bishop stood up and walked toward an empty spot in the room. He asked, "Come. Come."

They both did as they were asked, and found themselves standing hand in hand in front of a Bishop, who stood there holding a bible with two rings stacked on it. He wore a simple night shirt, instead of the normal celebratory robe he would wear for such an event. The bishop handed the bible to Father Henry for a moment while he wrapped the lace around their hands and asked them to kneel. They did so. Without opening the bible, he recited a prayer in Latin and then crossed himself. Father Henry, William, and Ainslee followed suit.

The first light of day crept over the western horizon as Bishop Emmanuel, William, and Ainslee loaded up into Father Henry's carriage. The carriage was only used to carry caskets and members of the grieving family from the church to the graveside. Outside of that, it sat beside the church and gathered dust, pollen, and leaves. It squeaked and shuddered as he signaled the horse to go. Not the most covert mode to sneak the newly-married couple and his guest out of town, but he planned to be out of town before anyone would be awake to hear the noise of the carriage. There was a good chance he could be back before anyone knew he was gone. The port town of Burwick was only six miles away.

Ainslee watched out the windows as everything she knew passed by. The grip she had on William's hand tightened as all of that slipped behind them and out of sight. They were on their way to a new life, and a new beginning. That was when it dawned on her, she didn't know where this new life took them. "So, where are we going?", she asked her new husband.

"Italy. Vatican City," said Bishop Emmanuel.

14

William and Ainslee had set off on a great adventure to see the world. For the last two weeks, all they'd seen was the ocean, with the occasional hint of shoreline in the distance, but most of the time it was water, water, and more water. Water that turned from dark blue into a light turquoise, a sign that Bishop Emmanuel said meant they were close to their destination.

The two newlyweds were inseparable. At night, they did what newlyweds did. Ainslee's presence on the voyage was not expected, but at the bishop's request, the crew had made arrangements so they would have a room all to their own. By day, they were together on the deck, basking in the sun and warmer temperatures, something that was foreign to two people who'd spent their entire lives in a land that seemed to always be covered in a layer of fog. Only the private conversations between William and Bishop Emmanuel separated them. These conversations happened twice, sometimes three times, a day. William never spoke of them when he returned, no matter how much Ainslee probed.

On the morning of their fifteenth day at sea, the two of them laid in bed like they had on the previous fourteen days. The sun snuck in through the single window and shone on the wall across the room. William was awake first, as he usually was. The clock of a farmer was firmly planted in his soul. He didn't mind. It gave him time to lay there and watch his beloved sleep, to listen to her breathe. Part of him felt like this was all a dream. Weeks ago, it would not have been possible. Even if he had worked up the nerve to ask her father for permission to court Ainslee, he had no doubt such a request would have been rejected. Lord McLayer had to have a list of more suitable suitors in mind for his daughter. Now, she was there in his arms, and their future was ahead of them. The past still made an occasional tug. He thought of his farm, his animals, John, the smell of the morning dew at daybreak. It had an almost sweet aroma to him. What he had woken up to the last two weeks, was, well... salty.

At first it seemed like any of the other previous mornings on board, but a sound caught William's attention. It wasn't the creaks and groans of the wood planks of the ship. Those were all normal, and had almost become a part of his essence and unnoticeable. Above them, on deck, there was a rush of activity. William slid out of bed and slipped on his pants. He walked out the door and up the stairs into the bright sun of the morning. His head breached the opening and he looked around.

"Mr. Miller, good morning," said Captain Leonardiz. The salty old man, with a beard as black as coal, was missing something. The scowl that always appeared plastered to his face was not there. A smile was in its place. "Welcome to Civitavecchia."

William turned toward the bow, where the hive of activity was. Men pulled ropes and dropped the sails of the foremast and mizenmast. Others loosened up the sail on the main mast, letting air out of the great white sail. In the distance, beyond the crew, there was something he hadn't seen in over two weeks. Land.

William rushed down the stairs and exploded into the room he and Ainslee shared. She was still asleep until the door slammed behind it and he exclaimed, "We are here!"

Ainslee rustled awake and looked at him from underneath the covers. With a yawn she asked, "What?"

"We are in Italy. Well, not in, but coming close. I can see it. It is close. Right out there. Ahead of us," William said, speaking faster than his betrothed could hear.

"William. What are you trying to tell me?", she asked, now leaning up on an arm as she watched her husband get dressed.

He took a breath and then tried again to explain, "We are approaching land. We are in Italy."

This statement was made as clear as a bell, one that went off with a loud dong in her head. She rushed up out of the bed and splashed two handfuls of water from the wash basin onto her face. Using the same linen she had used for the last two weeks, she pulled it across her face to remove the water and grime. No time to attempt a bath before donning the same dress she had worn since they'd left. It had been rinsed out a few times, that had removed a few stains and any smells, but it was anything but what one would describe as fresh. A quick swipe backward through her hair with a brush pushed her beautiful red locks behind her ears and shoulders. With her shoulders back, she exited the door. Her husband hopped around a few steps before his right foot slipped into his boot.

Up on deck, Ainslee rushed forward, bumping into several crew members on her way. Her face lit up like it was Christmas morn as she gazed out on the approaching view. In the distance, features began to take shape. The masts of tall ships already anchored in port stood just beyond a large stone structure. She pointed it out to William, who had joined her at the bow. The closer they came, the more features of the city came into view. It was larger than St. Margaret's Hope, much larger.

"That is Fortress Michangelo," Bishop Emmanuel said, in his rich Italian accent. William wasn't sure why, but that phrase itself sounded more sophisticated than any phrase he had heard in his life. "Pope Julius II built it over a hundred and fifty years ago to protect his fleet and the economy of the region."

"I am going to guess this is not a fishing village?"

The bishop leaned against the rail and faced William as he responded to his last statement. "No, not at all. This port is the Pope's private military fleet, and the primary exporter of alum. There is a large deposit of it just to the north."

Both William and Ainslee looked at each other. William didn't want to seem ignorant to someone who had put such great faith in him, but he had no clue what alum was. It was a substance he had never heard about. Neither of them needed to ask the question, though. Their tour guide could guess at the question by the looks on their faces. He volunteered, "It's a crystal that can be ground up and used in the tanning of leathers, as well as some medicines."

Both mouthed "oh" and acted like this was common knowledge they should be aware of.

Captain Leonardiz anchored the ship about a hundred yards offshore. From this vantage point, William and Ainslee could see everything. The Mediterranean buildings lining the shoreline. Hundreds of people moved in and around the port, which were more than either of them had ever seen in a single place before. More ships in a single place they either of them had ever seen, as well. If all the fishing boats in St. Margaret's Hope were in port at the same time, they would have to double, or even triple them, to match. Even in those numbers, they wouldn't equal this sight. Those were just small boats, what was in port with them here were great ships, with large masts and huge sails. Some just plain white. Others with various symbols on them, keys and crosses.

"Come. Come," Bishop Emmanuel said as he walked back toward midship. Three members of the crew were lowering a longboat into the water. The old and frail-looking Bishop flung himself up on the railing and then quickly descended a rope ladder into the boat waiting below. Both William and Ainslee gave the ladder a questionable look.

"You first, " said William.

The cockeyed look from Ainslee told him she disagreed.

"I mean, you go first. I will help you down from here." William reached out for her hand. She sat on the rail and swung her feet over. William held her left hand and right shoulder to steady her. "Now turn around. You need to go down facing the ship."

"What?!?"

"Put your foot down on that ledge, and turn toward me. I will hold you the whole way."

"Don't let me fall!", she warned.

William promised, "I won't."

She turned while William maintained two hands on her. Holding her right hand as he bent over the railing, Ainslee made it down the ladder and into the boat. William followed shortly after, with an attempt intended to be as graceful as the

Bishop, but a misstep on the last rung sent his boot crashing down on the bottom of the long boat with a thud. Neither the Bishop nor the oarsman were amused. His wife, on the other hand, was and smirked before exploding into laughter.

In just a few minutes the oarsman delivered his three passengers to the harbor's wharf. The three departed from the boat, and two of them stood, frozen, while the third member continued walking through a grand archway. The bishop never stopped to wait for the other two, he continued through the large stone archway of the Livorno Door. Neither William nor Ainslee had seen such a thing. It was massive, with people coming in and out at a dizzying pace. The opening looked large enough to fit their church, St. Margaret's Hope's largest building, inside, spiral and all. "*How could anyone build something so tall?*", he wondered. Did they have a tall ladder? William remembered how queasy he had felt climbing up his ladder to make roof repairs. It would shake and shudder with every step. Not to mention the one time he fell off when it slipped, he landed with an awful thud. To reach the top, you would need something ten times taller. That was a job he knew he didn't want.

William's focus shifted from the structure, to the opening itself. It was impressive, but missing something. Bishop Emmanuel. He grabbed his wife's hand and rushed through the people and then through the door. Her eyes and head craned to take it all in as her husband pulled her along. He said, "Excuse me," as they bumped into or cut people off. Each responded with a look of confusion and annoyance. Some exclaimed, using words that he didn't understand. He knew people in other countries spoke other languages, this was the first time he had experienced it, it didn't come with the sense of wonder he expected it would. Instead, he felt very small, alone, and confused.

A sigh of relief pulled some of that feeling out of him, when he spied their guide, Bishop Emmanuel, just ahead of them, next to a horse drawn carriage on a cobblestone road. A single driver, clothed in a red uniform, was mounted on the front of the solid black coach. He sat upright, with the leads in his hands. The door, embossed with two crossed gold keys, was held open by a man in a yellow and blue striped uniform, with a metal helmet adorned with a red plume. A long pike was held straight up by his other hand. The bishop entered the coach first. When William and Ainslee reached it, he held her hand again to help her inside. The coach lurched to the side a little when William entered, another instance that seemed to amuse his wife. Before he sat down, the door slammed shut behind him. There were a few lurches back and forth, which William assumed was the guard climbing up next to the driver, and then a lunge forward and they were off. Bishop Emmanuel leaned back and closed his eyes. William and Ainslee, couldn't if they tried. Each were attached to a window, taking in the sights and sounds of the city they rolled through, toward the Italian countryside.

15

The coach rumbled forward into the night. Two of its three passengers were fast asleep. Why shouldn't they be? It had been a long voyage, and a long day in the coach, but that wasn't it. William and Ainslee were used to hard work and long days. Their exhaustion was rooted in overstimulation. The world they had known all of their lives had just been put in perspective. It was miniscule, like the tip of a pin, in the grand scheme of things. There was a world full of wonders out there, unlike anything either of them could have imagined. The one person in the coach that was awake understood that. While he sat there, still, with his eyes closed. He was not asleep, but instead just relaxing and giving his two guests a moment alone, as alone as they could be in the small coach, to enjoy it together. That was why he disturbed their peaceful rest.

"Ainslee. William." He nudged each one with the softness of a parent waking a sleeping child.

Both rustled awake, stretched, and looked around in the coach, confused. Bishop Emmanuel simply pointed to direct their attention out the windows. Both turned and leaned toward the window closest to them. What they had seen of the world so far hadn't prepared them for this. Line upon line of gas lamps lined the cobblestone streets. Buildings of marble, with ornate architecture, decorated with gold, bronze, and other precious metals, were everywhere. These were no simple stone homes with thatch or wood-clad roofs. William's mind searched for the word to describe it. The one it came up with was luxurious.

"William, what is that?"

The same question echoed in his head as the coach pulled into the plaza. The sound of water bubbling down a brook accentuated the tranquil night, but there was no brook to be seen. Ainslee was fascinated by this and stood up to lean out the window to look around. When she found the sources, she reached over and tapped William, but he didn't notice. He couldn't. His eyes had caught sight of the structure in the center of the plaza, it was some sort of tower that went up as far as he could see. As fascinating as that was to him, it only held his attention for a second as the enormity of the building behind it emerged from the darkness and into view. It filled the skyline from side to side, and was highlighted by row upon row of lanterns. On the top of it was a great dome. As he took it all in, he noticed there were no other streets leading out. His mind asked, *"Were they on the steps of heaven, itself?"* If so, behind the golden doors he saw at the top of the stairs that led up from the plaza would be Saint Peter himself.

"That is the Obelisk of Saint Peter's. It was brought here from Egypt over 1700 years ago," explained Bishop Emmanuel as they passed by the large statue.

William only half heard him. The name Saint Peter resonated inside. It agreed with what his mind had thought, but that would mean one thing. They, Emmanuel, Ainslee, and himself, had passed on, but when? Maybe the ship ran into a storm and all on board had perished. The remainder of the voyage was to deliver their souls. If that were the case, shouldn't he remember the storm? William didn't consider himself an expert on the afterlife, but he did have more *experience* with it than most, if you excluded his present company. Something he realized early on was that those who had appeared to him always appeared confused. A feeling he now shared. Now, the few times he had tried to understand the what, why, and how of what he saw and could do, he was never really sure if they were confused, or if that was just how he perceived it. Not that it was something he thought about often. There was no way for him to know for sure. They never responded to him when he had tried to talk to them, so he couldn't simply ask, not that he hadn't tried enough times. If this were true, it would also explain why he hadn't seen any ghosts since they'd left, that was the longest he had ever gone without a sighting.

As William considered their fate, and Ainslee searched for the source of the water, the coach's wooden wheels clattered on the cobblestones through the plaza before coming to a stop in front of the stairs. The coach shuddered left and then right, before settling back on its springs with a few smaller bounces. The door opened, and the navy and yellow-clad guard appeared. He stood at attention as Bishop Emmanuel stepped out. He turned to the two remaining passengers and said, "Welcome to Saint Peter's Basilica, the Vatican, and your home for the next few months."

"You mean, we aren't dead?", asked William.

The pinched expression and narrow eyes on Bishop Emmanuel's face made William feel sheepish. He was not amused as he turned and continued up the stairs.

William stepped out and then helped his wife down out of the coach. Hand in hand, they followed the bishop up the stairs and through the large golden doors. Inside, they stepped on glossy marble floors. William took a few quick high steps. expecting the floor to be covered in a thin layer of water. With his eyes on the painted ceilings high above his head, this produced a stumble revealing the grace of a foal taking its first steps. Bishop Emmanuel appeared unfazed by their surroundings and continued down the hall.

They followed him as close as they could, having to jog a few times to catch up after their attention was distracted by a painting on the wall, a vase on a stand, or just the sheer beauty of the illuminated space around them. Their footsteps echoed through the halls like explosions. He turned down a hallway where the lanterns were more spaced out, creating pockets of darkness. In front of them, the bishop disappeared into one of those pockets and then reappeared, only to disappear again. An eerie unsettling feeling overcame William each time he walked through a pocket of darkness. The squeeze on his hand told him Ainslee felt it too. He squeezed back to reassure her.

It was in one of these pockets of darkness where, if it were not for the blast of light coming from the side, they would have walked right into the bishop. He stood in the center of the hall, in front of an open door, a door he directed both of them through. They entered, he did not.

The room was quaint, compared to the hallway they'd just left. A large bed sat against the far wall, which was painted white like the others. In front of a large fireplace, with a bronze mesh hanging over the opening, was a table with two chairs. Neither of which were simple wooden chairs like William had at home, both the back and seats had cushions.

"William. Get some rest. I will send for you in the morning," Bishop Emmanuel said, just before the door closed behind them.

When the door closed, Ainslee danced around the room. There was no music, but she didn't need it. She floated from space to space, looking at everything. The table. The draperies, something neither of them had seen before. William's tired body and mind were focused on the bed. It looked soft and warm, something neither his back home, nor the one they'd shared on the ship, were. A screech from the attached room sent him running. Inside the white-tiled room was Ainslee, her hands over her mouth, eyes focused on a large tub. Water ran out of a spout into the tub. William walked toward it and passed his hand through the water, his fingers played in the stream falling from the spout. Ainslee stepped forward and turned the silver handle on top of the spout, and the water stopped. She giggled like a little girl chasing a butterfly in the Scottish meadows.

William walked back out into the main room, mind wandering. His wife followed behind him and finally asked a question she hadn't asked in the two weeks since they'd left the only home either of them had ever known.

"William, why are we here?"

16

"Please tell me this is some kind of sick joke," Ainslee begged as she laid back on the bed and stared up at the ceiling above her. It wasn't a plain flat one, but a beautiful one, a work of art made of moldings and paint. She hadn't undressed before she laid down. This was not a time for sleep for her, or for William. What her husband had just explained to her had made her feel woozy, and she almost fell in the center of the room. He caught her before she hit the floor and pulled her to the bed. The lightheaded feeling she felt passed as she laid back, but the color had yet to return to her face.

"I wish it was. I had hoped for years it was, but it isn't," William said as he paced at the foot of their bed. Inside, his stomach did backflips. It would have been foolish for him to believe he could keep this hidden from her. At some point he would slip up, or she would become curious and ask about their situation, like she had now. The fact that she hadn't asked during their two-week long voyage gave him a little hope he would have more time to figure out how.

"How long has Father Henry known about your... ability?"

"Only a few weeks, but I believe my father was like me, and he knew about him. I am not sure really."

"Bishop Emmanuel is going to train you in what exactly?"

"To be honest, I'm not sure," said William. He was being truthful. During their one conversation, the bishop had never gone into any great detail in explaining what he would be training him in. He had never asked, either, which in hindsight was a more than a bit foolish. The offer to leave and pursue anything the outside world presented, had hit him in his heart, leaving his mind out of the decision. Looking back on it, the second thoughts were what probably triggered that nightmare he had had. "Something about knowing how to deal with them and to protect the living," he added.

"Ok. This must be real," she said.

William was preparing to try to explain again, but stopped mid-thought. The pacing stopped, and everything in his mind left, except one question, *"What did she just say?"*

"Look at the efforts they went through to bring you here, and look at where we are. We are in the Vatican, the center of everything that is spiritual." Ainslee was sitting up now, propped on her elbows, her color was returning, but not quite back yet. She patted the bed next to her and said, "He said you start in the morning. You'd better get your sleep, ghost warrior."

The wry smile on her face made William leery. It was one he had seen one too many times. That look always ended with him either being pushed off the wall, slugged in the arm, or the butt of her own joke. She and John had always found those jokes hilarious, William, not so much. Her sense of humor was one of the traits he loved about her, but it also cut sharp and deep. Once, when they were barely ten years old, she led him out, away from the farmland he was familiar with, and into the adjacent forest. They had gone in deep, turning here and there. William felt lost, but he wasn't overly concerned. It was obvious that Ainslee knew where she was going.

They slowed as they had reached a tree with a trunk that twisted around. She told him that the tree was magical, if you kissed someone under it, your dreams would come true. William was told right where to stand and he did, eyes closed, and lips puckered, then he heard giggling. When he opened his eyes, he saw Ainslee's hair blowing in the wind behind her as she ran away from him. He tried to follow, but his feet were stuck. Where she had him stand was a patch of moor mud. Stuff so thick and strong it could trap a horse. Being only ten, he was nowhere close to the strength of a horse.

William screamed and screamed. First for her to come back, then for anyone within ear shot. The combination of the cold damp air and his screaming had caused his voice to go raw and raspy. When it was nothing more than a whisper, she came back. Tears rolled down his cheeks. That devious wry smile was on her face then, too. He expected her to make fun of him, or to take off running again, now in the other direction. Perhaps she would leave him out there all night and only come back when forced to lead his parents to where she had left him. In truth, he hadn't known what to expect. What had happened next, wouldn't have made it on the list if he had made one. She leaned in and kissed him. Softly and warmly, her hand dangling next to his and, for just the briefest of moments, she grabbed it. When she let go of his hand, and his lips, she helped him ease his legs out of the moor mud and walked him home, soggy boots and all. There had been no apology, he didn't need one. From that point on, things had changed. Maybe that legend was true, look where they are now.

There was no further conversation for the night. Ainslee's eyes drew heavy and closed. Her breathing slowed to a restful rhythm. The sound of that soothed William and sent him off to sleep, as well. The next sound he heard was a knock on the door. At first, William laid there and didn't move. When he heard the knock for a third time, he sat up. Pools of sunlight splashed across the room, through the gaps in the draperies. It was a good thing too, the light helped him see a few things, limiting what he bumped into on his way to the door. He just missed bumping into a chair at a bureau, and a footstool at the end of the bed. As he opened it, a young girl, no more than fifteen or sixteen years old, wearing an all-white habit, stood at the door, her head looking straight down at the golden tray she held.

Before William could say, "Morning", or ask what she needed, the girl walked in through the tiny space between the doorframe and William, and proceeded to the table in the center of the sitting section of the room. She placed her tray down, and then hurried out, never looking up from the floor. He walked out behind her and watched her walk at a brisk pace down the hall, her head never coming up, her feet never making an audible sound in the cavernous hall.

He walked back in and shut the door behind him. Then looked at the tray she had placed on the table. By now Ainslee was awake and sitting up in bed. Her eyes followed her husband as he tended to the door and inspected the tray. It had an assortment of bread and poached eggs, on a plate. Two cups held a brown liquid that William thought was coffee, based on the color and consistency. When he took a sniff of the steam that rose up from it, it was tea. Strong tea. He looked back at Ainslee and said, "Breakfast."

She sprang up off the bed and rushed over to the table. They were both famished. The coach had stopped twice to water and feed the horses. The driver, guard, and occupants had taken that opportunity to stop and have a bite to eat, as well, but the excitement and nerves of the day had burned off all their energy, they needed to resupply. They sat and ate, and afterwards took turns in the large porcelain tub with the fountain running into it. For the first time in days, they felt clean. They were only able to sponge off while on the ship. There was no proper bath, just a basin with some water. Ainslee found it better for washing their clothes than washing themselves.

Cleaned and dressed, they barely had a moment to wonder what was next for the day when there was another, much firmer, knock at the door. William opened it, and found Bishop Emmanuel standing on the other side, hands held near his waist, palms pressed together. There were no pleasantries. No "Good morning" or "How did you sleep?", just a firm "Come, William. We need to start your lessons."

William started out the door, but stopped as the bishop took a step inside. He turned toward where Ainslee stood looking out the window. "Ainslee, my dear. Sister Francine will be back shortly to take the tray and show you around. For the next several weeks, this is to feel like your home. Our city has a lot to offer." He turned and walked out the door beckoning, "Come, William."

Feeling more himself than he had over the last several days, William let a bit of his unsophisticated humor show through. "When is my tour of the city?"

Bishop Emmanuel retorted, "Oh, you will have plenty of opportunities to see the city. Most of them at night, when you will be most useful."

William didn't know if he was trying to answer humor with humor, or if he was serious.

17

William's parents made sure their son could read and write. Even with the plans of him taking over the family farm, they both saw those skills as necessary to conduct business, as well as to be a contributing member of society, so bookwork didn't concern him much. What was concerning during his first meeting with Bishop Emmanuel, was the volume and the content. They had set up a makeshift classroom at a table in a large library. All day long, the bishop gave instructions to monks and scribes, in Latin, who scurried away, up and down every aisle, searching the bookcases for what he had requested. William only caught a few names here and there.

One of the scribes was named Roberto, or that is what the bishop had called him once when he had retrieved the wrong text from the shelves, and he sent the short rotund balding figure back to search again. Another was Cristobal. He was different. Unlike the others, that would go off and search for what was requested. Cristobal not only returned with what he was sent for, but always had one or two more items in hand that he and the bishop took a few moments to review before adding them to the stack. A stack that grew by the moment, and was now totaling ten books, in all. When the eleventh was put on top of it, and the twelfth, one of Cristobal's recommendations, was put down to the side of the stack, the search was done. Much to the pleasure of the old priests in the opposite corner from them, who had grown rather irritated at all the moving around and interruptions to their silence.

Pulling two books from the stack, Bishop Emmanuel asked, "I am going to guess you don't read Latin?"

"I don't."

This news seemed to upset Roberto and the two other men, whose names William had not yet caught. Each appeared to be in their early thirties, and wore simple white smocks over black gowns. Cristobal responded by saying, "Riformatore." The others seemed to understand what he said and nodded in agreement. William had no clue and sat there with a blank expression on his face as the conversation occurred above his head. At least until Cristobal explained it to William.

"Pre-reformation, everyone knew Latin. It was the language of education, law, medicine, and the church. Where you are from, they separated the church, and everything," he stopped himself to correct the statement, "well, everything you would have been exposed to is now in your common language. There is nothing to worry about. I can translate for you."

His tone was warmer, friendlier, than the others'. Everyone else had what his father would call the 'cold business tone'. They were here to do a job, and that was all. Cristobal gave the impression of someone who wanted to help, which helped William breathe a huge sigh of relief. There was also something different, his accent was richer than the others'. William wondered where he was from. That would be something he would have to ask him at some point.

Bishop Emmanuel seemed pleased, as much as the man ever showed outwardly, that the young scribe had volunteered to help. So much so, he assigned him to be responsible for his academic training. That was a responsibility he didn't bat an eye about, as he slid his chair over next to William, dragging two books with him. The others left without a word. No indication of how long this would go on, or when they would be back. William watched as they left, as his teacher began the lesson.

"William, what do you know about life and death?"

The question was a seemingly simple one, which to William meant it deserved a similar answer. "Well, you are born and live, then you get old and die."

"Okay, in its crudest terms, yes, but what happens after you die?"

William thought about this for a second and considered where he was. In the Catholic Church there could only be one answer, and it was the same as the Anglican Church. "Your soul is welcomed into the ever after."

"Heaven, is that what you speak of?", asked Cristobal.

William nodded.

"Yes and no. Well… " he paused and gave an educated giggle, like a sleuth who had caught someone in a ruse, "that is what the Church wants you to think. It is the simplest and easiest view to accept. The truth is, we don't have a clue."

The surprise of such an admission, sitting here inside the holiest of holy buildings in the world, must have been written all over William's face, because Cristobal asked, "I take it that hearing that surprises you?"

Before William could answer, he continued to explain, "What you are going to learn, for as long as you are here, is not Church doctrine, beliefs, indoctrination, or anything else you might get as part of a sermon back home, or from the Holy Father, himself. You are going to learn the truth, or the truth as we know it or believe it to be. Some will be conjecture; some is what we have learned simply by doing. Some you are going to learn right alongside us. There are no set instructions on how to do what we are asking you to do. You have to figure out what works, and apply it. So, back to life and death. If it were as simple as you live, and then you die and go to heaven or hell, then why are there spirits that are still bound to this world?"

The question was not one Cristobal expected William to answer. He ended the question by opening a book to a page with a disturbing image on it. William didn't understand what he was looking at, but he knew it was evil. "In 1320, Italian poet Dante Alighieri completed a work that contained a view of the nine circles of hell. Each circle is a level you must pass through on your way into the underworld." His finger traced the page from the top down, each image more disturbing than the last. "Now, you may be thinking he was just a poet, and this was just a poem, but this work reflected a critical belief that was growing in the Church at that time." He flipped several pages to a similar diagram, that was less disturbing. "In addition to describing what you just saw in Inferno, he also wrote of the nine levels you must travel through to reach heaven, Paradiso." His finger now traveled from the bottom of the page, up through the images, to the top. "In between both is his second part, Purgatorio, or as you know it, Purgatory. Have you heard that term before?"

"Yes, that is the place where souls sit to suffer for all eternity. They neither go to heaven or hell." The sermons Father Henry gave were rarely fire and brimstone. Most where of an enlightening message, to give those that needed it hope, but occasionally he went dark with his message and used that image to help warn those in his congregation to not slip off what he called "the slick path of salvation".

"I bet you can see where this is going. Now, if you go strictly by the text, Purgatory is a mountain you have to climb to get to Paradiso, heaven, but you don't really start on that climb until you get through the first two levels called Ante-Purgatory. Those levels are called Excommunicate and Late Repentant. The last of which has a gate as an exit to the first level of true Purgatory. That is Saint Peter's Gate."

His teacher stopped the lecture for a moment and brought his brown eyes even with William's. A smile broke across his face as he saw the lightning bolt of knowledge strike inside his student. William sat back in his chair and looked up. His eyes looked up at the imagery depicted in the great stained glass windows that existed every few feet along the walls of the top level. Then he looked up at the fresco on the ceiling. The images, one after another, lined with details of what Cristobal had just explained to him.

"If it weren't for the ability of some of us to see and experience those souls trapped, we would think this was just a work of literature and a silly belief system. For now, it is the only thing that makes sense."

William asked, "So, how do we help them climb the mountain?"

"Oh, you are going to be great at this."

18

When William returned back to his and Ainslee's residence in the Vatican, he found it empty, which suited him fine. He was sure she would have a ton of questions about his first day of "training" and at the moment, he was more exhausted than any day out in the pasture had ever made him. His body wasn't tired, though, it was his mind. The result of six straight hours, scouring book after book, most of it in Latin, which required Cristobal to explain it to him. Most William understood right away, but some of the finer points required additional explanation.

Their studies covered the theories of life and death, combined with documented studies of spirits and groups of spirits that priests, and others like William, had encountered. Each study appeared to take what they'd observed and tried to fit it into their current view. At first this was a shock to William. They, those he thought were experts, didn't have a true understanding of what they were doing. This was all just guessing, based on their current beliefs and what they had observed. What was comforting was how candid Cristobal was about it all. William had expected a member of the church to be locked and rigid about their beliefs and how things were, but he was far from it. He was almost logical and scientific in his approach. He took the time to show him the times they'd had to rethink their understanding, to emphasize that it was an ever-evolving topic. Where a high level of uncertainty existed, he pointed it out.

He walked William through the study of Friar Benedictor, a Franciscan monk that, like William, could see them. The friar had had unusual and fortunate encounters with a repeating visitor. After he encountered and contacted the same spirit, in the same spot on the grounds of the monastery, for the third time, he decided to test a theory. Each time he saw the spirit, it roamed up to the courtyard wall and turned, only to encounter the wall on the other side and then turned again. It would repeat this, over and over. Being that the monastery was holy grounds, he hypothesized that spirits are sensitive to holy objects and people. He placed objects in the courtyard, both blessed and not, as his test and control variables. Two nights later, his test subject arrived, and he watched. As always, it wandered around between the walls, but never attempted to avoid any of the objects he had placed around the courtyard, whether they were blessed or not. Concerned his test subject may not be aware of anything but the walls, the friar walked into the courtyard, toward the spirit. When he was close enough, the spirit retreated away from him, several feet. He repeated this several more times, backing the spirit into a corner of the courtyard, against the wall. The friar reached out with his hand and touched it once again, and the spirit disappeared through the very wall he believed had trapped it in the courtyard. What he learned was, they were not aware of objects that had no importance to them, whether it was blessed or not. To provide supporting details to his conclusion, he tried to determine who the spirit was, and why they might be connected to the courtyard. He didn't have to go far, just another hundred yards to the cemetery, where he found the headstone of Friar Montgomery, who died eighty years earlier, and had constructed that very courtyard wall.

The friar's findings were gathered and delivered to the Council of Zion, an eleven member board made up of clergy and cardinals, that reviewed any such findings for correctness and completeness. If any beliefs needed to be adjusted based on a report, this group made such adjustments.

Thoughts and images of his learnings danced in his head as he laid back on the lush bedding. His brain craved sleep, to recover from the day's activities, as well as to process all he had learned. His eyes closed, but the outside world was not replaced by darkness. Instead, pages of text and images raced across his vision, and around in his subconscious. His mind was too tired to make an attempt to comprehend, and let the pages fall into the emptiness below while he retreated further and further into the darkness of sleep.

William woke up minutes, or hours, later to a huge racket in the sitting area of their residence. He leaned up and expected to find Ainslee, perhaps sitting there drinking tea after her day out, but that was not the case. The heat coming off his visitor, blistering his skin, told him who was there before he opened his eyes. The flames around him seemed larger than they had back during the dream in his home. Maybe it wasn't a dream after all.

"I see you didn't listen to me," thundered the familiar coarse voice. Its yellow eyes seemed more focused and determined this time. "You really should have listened. You had such a great future ahead of you. A wonderful family. Year after year of bountiful harvests. All given up, for what? The promise of something greater, by a bunch of old men that play dress-up. The life this leads to is nothing like the one I offered. The road to their greatness is paved with pain and sorrow."

It picked up one of the teacups Ainslee had left on the table, and mimicked taking a sip before placing it back on the table with a thud, then stood up from the table. Its hooves clopped against the tile floor as it walked around the table and over to the footstool William had kicked earlier that morning. When it reached the stool, it sat and crossed one leg over the other. Its hands were placed on top of its knee as it leaned forward. Its posture mimicked one he had seen Bishop Emmanuel take once, when he was lecturing William about the responsibility he was being entrusted with, during their discussions on board the ship.

"Now, I could just condemn you for ignoring my offer, but I am not a vengeful creature. It is not too late, William. You and your cherry of a wife could return home, your real home, not this place, and have all that I offered."

"Why should I believe you?", William asked.

"You can talk. I was beginning to think you were a mute. That is a fair question. Why should you believe me?", It brought a flame-engulfed hand up to its chin and rubbed, while deep in thought. Sparks flew from its fingertips with each stroke. Then it snapped its fingers, producing more sparks. "That's right. I can do what I promise, and they can't, it is that simple."

It sat there and watched William from the footstool, its yellow eyes probing below the skin and into the essence of the man. A series of images flowed through his mind: the farm, with fields full of lush green crops; two large young boys helping him put up a new fence; Ainslee, looking on with the smile of an angel on her face. Each image reinforced the promise the creature had made. Each image also brought a sense of contentment, happiness, and pleasure to William. A fresh spring breeze, with a hint of early morning dew, replaced the heat that radiated from the flames that surrounded the creature. Chill bumps developed on his arms.

"I will come back for my answer," it said, and dissipated into a puff of steam as the door opened.

Ainslee burst in, all aglow, "You are back," she exclaimed. She was followed by the same young woman, in a white habit, that had come in with breakfast that morning. Her gaze was no longer focused on the floor but, instead, was up and confident. The plain, blank, almost subservient look she had possessed earlier was gone, replaced by a pleasant smile. Ainslee rushed over to hug and kiss her husband. Over her shoulder, William noticed that the nun had turned to give them privacy for their show of affection.

"The city is beautiful. Fountains, churches, shops, everywhere. It is like walking through paradise, with all the beautiful buildings, and … oh, the food. I didn't eat any, mind you, but the smells that roll up and down the street are enough to make your mouth water."

While Ainslee gushed over her tour of Vatican City, and the surrounding area of Rome, her escort stood in the sitting room. The pleasant look that was on her face when she had walked in was gone. One of concern had replaced it as she walked around the table. Her eyes moved from the chair the creature had sat in, up to the ceiling, and down again. Then, as she walked toward the footstool, the look of concern grew to despair. Her eyes became jittery as she approached the stool. She passed her right hand through where the creature had sat, and then ran back to the center of the room, hand over her mouth as she gasped out loud.

19

If William's head wasn't tired and spinning after his day of reading and training, it was after Ainslee's whirlwind recap of her day in town. She took her husband on a descriptive tour of each and every street she had traveled. Some of it was just her telling him, but others were even more enjoyable for William. She bought slices of bread, cheese, and meat, rolled up in a cloth. Flowers of various sweet fragrances were rolled up in another. Sister Francine explained that people placed them in vases in their residences to add a floral fragrance to the air, and once they started to wilt you could pluck the petals and add them to your bath water to create an aromatic perfume that would stay on your skin for days. William thought it odd that a nun would be aware of such an indulgence, but just because she knew about it didn't mean she practiced it. The audible tour continued for the rest of the afternoon, until Sister Francine returned with their dinner on a tray. She carried another object on her tray, as well, a vase.

So far, the outside world was meeting, if not exceeding, her wildest dreams. William, on the other hand, had seen a ship and the inside of a library. Albeit an impressive library, as was every other room and hall he had seen in the Vatican. The food wasn't bad, either. Everything was cooked just right, and the flavors were an experience. Meat that tasted sweet, vegetables that had an oily spice to them, and the bread! The bread had a buttery flavor to it, without any butter in sight.

William's fork hit the plate for the last time, when there was a knock at the door. After another quick swig of red wine from his chalice, he wiped his mouth with a small linen that was next to his plate and pushed away from the table. When he opened the door, he saw Cristobal and Bishop Emmanuel. Behind them, two monks stood in full brown robes, hoods pulled up over their heads. Their hands crossed at the center of their body. Both held a lit lantern in their hands.

"William, you need to come with us," said Bishop Emmanuel.

"More training?", he asked.

Cristobal said, "Something like that."

William walked out the door and noticed another member of their party standing outside the glow of the lanterns. He was diminutive compared to the others, and wore a red robe. His face was hidden among the shadows, and he turned away before William could get a good look. The man walked down the hallway, ahead of the rest of the group, and always outside the glow of the light. They retraced the steps

William and Ainslee had taken the night before, when they'd arrived, and descended the steps down to the plaza. At the bottom, no coach waited for them, wherever they were going, they were going on foot.

The night was quiet and cool. Only a handful of people were out walking in the streets, and the faint sound of music radiated from a few of the buildings as they walked north, away from St. Peter's Basilica. These streets were similar to the ones they'd rode in on last night, but as awe-inspiring as they were when seen from the coach, seeing them up close, like he was now, revealed them in more detail. Smooth rock walls. Ornate iron gates and railings that led to equally ornate doors, or covered the bottom half of second story windows, to create a balcony. What he didn't see were simple stone structures. With the exception of large structures, like churches and government buildings, and a few houses of the very well off, every building back home was made of simple stacked stone, or wood walls and thatched or shingled roofs. That was not the case here. Everything was an elegant stone structure, with decorative architectural features, and flat or red terra cotta roofs.

Their small leader in red broke his silence and said in a thick accent, "Non è molto più lontano."

Cristobal leaned into William and, just above a whisper, repeated what was said, but in English, "It's not much further."

"What isn't?"

20

"*Not far was right,*" thought William, as the group turned down a dark alleyway between two rows of three-story, peach-colored, stone buildings. There were no gas lanterns on poles lighting this passageway, just the ones carried by the two monks, several feet ahead of him. Which is why the appearance of stairs going down caught him a little off guard, and almost sent him tumbling, but he caught his first misstep and made it down the rest of the way without incident or embarrassment.

The stairs ended on another street much like the one they had left to go down the alley, but the lighthearted amazement William felt from his first up-close look at the city had been replaced by a familiar sense of dread, and a prickling along his neck. He knew what this was, without anyone saying a word. Knowing what he was here to do, William marched forward to take the lead and handle it, but he only made it two steps before Cristobal grabbed his arm and pulled him back to his place in line.

William looked at him with alarm, and was about to say something, when Cristobal said, "Just stand back and watch. You are not ready yet."

Those words stung a bit. This "gift" was not something William had just acquired. He had experience, a lot of it. If they didn't believe he was ready, then why did they bring him this far from home? His parents had instilled a sense of manners in their gruff and somewhat overconfident son, so he did as he was told. It would be rude to do anything other; he was their guest here.

Both William and Cristobal were cast into darkness as the two lantern-holding monks spread out to either side of their red-cloaked leader. Their arms panned the circles of light back and forth, in a slow progression. Every few swings of the light was followed by a step forward. Another few swings, and another step. This continued, but Cristobal didn't move forward with the lantern-swinging monks. He stayed put where he had stopped William from rushing forward, even as the light moved forward beyond them, he stayed, now bathed in darkness.

A low growl echoed down the narrow street. If that wasn't enough to send the hair on the back of William's neck standing on end, the fact that it came from behind them was. His fight or flight response was having an argument deep inside his mind. The urge to run was there, but why wasn't anyone else running, or even looking as if they were alarmed? Was he the only one who'd heard the growl?

He didn't give in to the urge to run, but did make an attempt to turn around and look for what was behind them.

"Don't," Cristobal warned at William's first attempt to turn. "Keep looking straight ahead, and when I tell you, clear the street."

William didn't ask for a clarification as the growl sounded again, this time closer, and this time it came with a vibration that shook the ground beneath his feet. Now he knew what Cristobal meant when he had said he wasn't ready yet. In all of his experiences, nothing had ever growled before, and definitely not shook the floor.

The growl echoed again, this time deeper, more primal, and it had company. It was not one growl, but several, contained in the same sound. A hot wind breathed on him from behind. Once again, his legs wanted to run, but he wouldn't let them. Not even when the hot breath moved back and forth across the back of his head, stirring several stray hairs. Chills coursed throughout his body. The world around him shook, causing his vision to vibrate. At first, he thought the shaking was caused by the great beast behind him moving back and forth, but his teeth chattered, revealing it was his body that shook. If William hadn't known what fear was before, he did now.

"William," said Cristobal. Each syllable strung out. There was a great pause that made William believe he was waiting on a reply. "NOW!"

Cristobal ran to the left, William's legs responded to the call and he ran to the right and pancaked himself up against the wall. The ground rumbled around them as the sound of some enormous beast snorting and running thundered past them. There was nothing there, not that William could see, but he could follow it by sound as it closed in on their red-cloaked leader. His eyes were trained on him, expecting him to get out of the way, but he didn't. The only move he made was to turn and throw off his hood, revealing the face of someone William would guess was eighty years old or more. That man's eyes squinted toward the beast, accentuating the age lines and wrinkles that dominated his face. He held up an object in his right hand and recited something, but William couldn't make out what the object was. It was too small, and the rumble beneath his feet shook his vision. The words he recited were muffled under the thundering steps of the beast, which showed no signs of slowing down as they rumbled toward and through the man, as he was thrown to the ground by a great impact.

It was at that one moment, for the briefest of seconds, that the beast came into view. It towered as tall as the three-story buildings that lined the street. Hooves the size of an entire horse, a body larger than William's farmhouse. Sitting on top of the shoulders was the head of a sneering and snorting man. The beast disappeared from sight again, but the sound of it coming to a stop further down the road and turning around was clear.

The two lantern-holding monks moved to help the man in red, but he waved them off as he stood and steadied himself in the center of the road. He turned toward the beast and began reciting something, this time louder. There was great passion in his voice as he spoke. From across the road, Cristobal translated for William

"Morax, the Great Earl, and President of Hell. You are in our world. We, under the power of Almighty God, have sole responsibility of the souls here, both living and dead. You are hereby ordered to leave this world, by the power of the Father, the Son, and the Holy Ghost."

The great beast charged again, but the man in red did not run. He steadied himself for this pass, once again holding a small object in his right hand, ready for the collision. The collision never came, not for the man in red. The beast veered off the road and gored one of the two lantern-holding monks, flinging him high into the air. The man in red leapt toward that side, not to aid the monk, but to make contact with the beast. When he did, it was visible again, as was the pain and agony it wailed about.

The man began reciting again, as the great beast was frozen in pain. The spot he touched with the object in his right hand seared its flesh.

Cristobal once again translated, this time missing parts, as much of what the man in red said was overpowered by the screams of the beast, "When Jesus had stepped out on land, there met him a man from the city who had demons. For a long time, he had worn no clothes, and he had not lived in a house but among the tombs..... He commanded the unclean spirit to come out of the man...." Cristobal stopped the translation once he recognized enough of it. "He is reciting verses from the book of Luke, chapter 8, verses 26, 27, and 28... he is continuing from the same book."

Cristobal was no longer translating, but reciting from memory, but William was no longer paying attention. The sight of the great beast engulfed in flames had taken that. It broke loose and barreled down the road, flames trailing behind it. The beast was no longer visible, but the flames that engulfed it were. It turned and charged the man again but, again, he didn't move. He waited, and as the great beast dipped its flaming head to deliver a blow to the man, he punched his right hand forward. A crack of thunder echoed through the clear sky. The beast didn't make it another inch. It dropped right there and moaned and wailed. Flames grew all over it. As the flames reached the head of a man on top of the great body, the wailing increased. A bluish smoke rose above the beast before it, the flames, and the smoke, disappeared into the darkness of the night.

The monk that had been thrown high in the air pushed himself up off the ground and retrieved his lantern before rejoining the other monk, behind the man in red. The three walked back in the direction they came from. When they reached William, Cristobal was standing in the road. He bowed and said something too silently for William to hear. The man turned toward William and walked in his direction.

When the four men reached him, Cristobal introduced him, "William, I want you to meet Cardinal Depeche. He is our most senior paranormal advocate."

The man in red held out his hand and William took it, bowed, and said. "It is a pleasure to meet you." The bow was out of respect, and a necessity in order to reach the man's hand at his height. William was still not sure what he had just witnessed. The ghosts he had seen had never looked or reacted like that. Question after question spun around in his mind.

It was obvious the cardinal didn't understand English, as Cristobal had to translate the simple greeting to him. William knew Cristobal would undoubtedly be the source, or at least the bridge, to the answers he searched for.

"What was that?"

The old man's voice cracked, "Morax."

"Morax, the Earl of Hell. He commands a legion of demons that try to enslave those souls stuck in our world. Occasionally they also make promises to those in the living world, in exchange for their souls. The cardinal has been battling those demons for years," Cristobal explained.

"So, is it over?"

"For now. He will be back. Think about it like this. We won the skirmish."

At that moment the image of a great battle of fire, on some mountaintop high above the clouds, leapt into his mind. Both the cardinal and the demon were chained to their spot. Neither able to leave. Destined to fight for all eternity. "That reading didn't get rid of him?"

"Oh, no. The reading was just that, a reading," explained Cristobal.

It was at that moment that the cardinal stepped forward and reached up to place his left hand on William's chest. In broken English he said in a voice so weak it appeared painful to talk, "The words... they provide you focus. The power comes from here." He took his hand off his chest, and returned to the road. The two globes of light caused by the lanterns carried by the two monks soon joined him as they headed back down the road toward the dark stairs they had descended earlier. Cristobal fell in line behind them.

William joined the parade and asked Cristobal, "What is that in his right hand?"

"It's a relic. We will cover that in a few days. I understand one of Morax's legions has been visiting you."

21

The walk back to the Vatican provided Cristobal another opportunity to teach, and expose William to a world that was even more complicated then he knew. Ghosts, or spirits as his teachings called them, were one thing, they were simple. Before now, he though demons were just a creation of scripture and fear, to drive a message to the congregation. The possibility that the creatures Cristobal was describing existed in their world was hard to fathom. Creatures, here, that worked with and manipulated people to do their bidding, all for the promise of knowledge, profit, love, or any other desired possession or achievement.

Cristobal explained that William was being targeted by one such demon. Sister Francine had sensed it in his residence and reported back. She was also sensitive to such creatures, but was not able to see or interact with them. William explained how it first appeared to him, the night before he left Scotland, and then again, here. He told him of the promise it had made. The lifetime of perfect crops, and the perfect healthy family. He nodded as he listened and then asked, "Were you tempted?"

"No. The first time I thought it was just a weird dream."

That response made his teacher chuckle. He then asked, "How did you feel when it made you the promises?"

William had to think about that for a moment. Both times there was a sense of contentment and pride, as the images replayed in his head. It was the life he longed and hoped for. Seeing it there, in imagery that felt as real as life itself, made it all feel possible. The first time it happened, he wasn't aware of what it was, though, and dismissed it as a wild dream, fueled by all the time he spent over the previous few days thinking of his experiences with spirits, and Bishop Emmanuel's offer to train him. The lack of any additional details provided by the bishop about his offer left a lot of gaps for his brain to fill in. William had always had a vivid imagination as a child, something he once chalked up as the explanation for the spirits he saw. If you give that kind of imagination enough gaps to fill, of course it could create that type of imagery and sensations. Now that he knows what he knows, the encounter becomes a little more chilling. The second time, he was aware it was real, but didn't know it was a demon, or even that they were real, yet. Now that he does, it changes everything, and he confessed, "It frightens me now. Why is he coming to me?"

"We will get to that. First, were you frightened at the time?"

"No," said William.

"Why not?"

"I didn't think the first time was real."

Cristobal then asked, "And the second?"

"A little, when he first appeared."

"So, let me ask you this. A demon with the bottom half of an animal, the top half of a man, surrounded in fire, appeared to you, why were you not scared out of your skin?" Cristobal turned to look at his student and walked backwards down the road, his eyes trained on him for his response.

That was a question William hadn't considered, and it showed on his face, producing another chuckle from his teacher.

"You don't know, do you?", he asked.

William shook his head as he continued to think about it. *Why wasn't he?*

Cristobal explained, "Nobody does. The archives are full of interviews taken of those that have seen demons, and not a single person was afraid. There is a reason. Demons are master manipulators." Cristobal smacked his hands together to emphasize that point. He turned and walked side by side with William. The tone of his voice contained a weight that it hadn't had through any of their studies, nor at any time earlier in the night. "That is something you must remember. Spirits don't manipulate you. They are what you see, and that is it. Never trust what you feel, hear, or see when a demon is present." His left hand slapped William on the chest as they walked. "Tell me you understand that."

"I understand," William said. His voice trailed off a bit and had a question mark hanging at the end. That question mark was attached to the question he asked before Cristobal continued, "Then h...how do you deal with demons?"

"First, you will not deal with demons. That is a priest's job, but that is not to say you will never encounter them. You will, and when you do, you go with what we are teaching you. It will never fail you. The challenge is in forcing your mind to ignore everything else, to not be taken in by them. The images it showed you, how did you feel when it showed them to you?"

"Happy."

"I bet you felt the warm sun on your face. A beautiful scent of some type wafting through the air around you, and images of your loved ones all smiling. Does that about cover it?"

As they mounted the steps to the Vatican, William nodded his head to answer his teacher.

"Of course, and let me tell you why. If someone is afraid, they won't listen to what it has to say. They need you to feel comfortable, or whatever emotion they need you to feel, to believe what they are trying to tell you."

Cristobal stopped at the top of the steps and continued, his voice a little lighter, warmer, than before. The hard edges that were present in his words of the last few minutes were gone, as he recalled his story. "A demon once came to me. It basically promised me the world. I was dressed in a black robe, with a crucifix around my neck, standing at the rose-line of a great church. Thousands were seated in the pews, repeating the prayer that I was leading. There, seated among my flock, was my father." His voice grew quieter, and dripped with remorse, "He smiled at me." Cristobal paused and looked out at St. Peter's obelisk before he took a large prolonged breath. "The demon showed me two things that would never be. My father never approved of my choice to be here. I was to follow him as a blacksmith. He would never be sitting there smiling, and there would never be a flock for him to sit among."

William knew Cristobal was not a priest. Instead, he was some sort of scholar, but he assumed he was training and learning to become one, based on the respect and how involved he was with his own training. "I don't understand. Are you not training to be a priest?"

"Let's have a seat here on the steps. It is a nice night out and sometimes I come to sit here and gaze at the plaza and ponder. My form of meditation, I guess."

The two sat, and William understood why this was his favorite spot. The great plaza was illuminated by the flickering gas lanterns that lined its borders under a clear star-filled night sky was a sight that matched, if not exceeded, in its own way, a clear cool spring night in the highlands around his home. The glow of the lights danced on the mighty stone obelisk that appeared to be standing guard overall.

"William, I cannot be a priest. The church would never allow it. I was married and a father. I was also not a very religious man. My focus was my family." He emphasized the word family in a way that made his accent stronger than at any other time William had heard. "They were taken from me, by something I didn't understand. The search for the truth brought me here. You see, my son became ill and what I now know was a demon, approached my wife with the promise of saving our son, in return he wanted her to be his agent of mischief in our realm. First, she ransacked the community crops one night. Then she released all the livestock from our neighbor's farm. Each time, she was found where these things happened and gave the excuse that she saw what happened and was trying to stop it. She gave wild descriptions of those she had seen running through the crops, or opening the doors, but no one was ever found. One night she was caught standing with a flaming torch next to a large pile of harvested grain, at a farm on the other side of town. I wasn't even aware she had left the house. When the farmer approached her, she screamed something at him in a language he didn't know and tried to touch the torch to the grain. He tackled her to the ground and, with the help of others in the area, dragged her in to town, to the constable. What he told me later was that when he laid eyes on her, her own eyes had gone solid black, and a green liquid spewed from her mouth. Every word she screamed was not one they recognized. He ordered the mob to take her to the priest, and he came to get me. By the time I arrived, Father Perez was trying to cleanse her soul, but she was fighting back. She had bent over in half, backwards, and screamed. I still hear that scream in my nightmares. It was full of woe and pain. There were multiple voices in it, screaming, but I could hear hers. I knew she was in pain, and suffering. I begged the priest to stop it, and I meant to stop both what he was doing, and what was happening to her. He continued and her legs and arms contorted around at unnatural angles until the bones snapped. She fell, lifeless, to the ground at the feet of the priest, in the middle of the mob that had brought her. Her body was twisted in so many ways, I couldn't even recognize her. When I returned home, I went to hold our son. His body was cold, death had come for him." A single tear rolled down Cristobal's cheek as he took several broken breaths.

"In the following days, Father Perez explained this world to me, and it made sense. I, like you, can see and sense ghosts. Always could. When I thought back on the days before Josefina started acting peculiar, I remembered I had felt something, but had dismissed it. I was blinded from seeing the truth, because of my lack of knowledge of this side of it, and my feelings for her. When I realized that, I committed my life to finding the truth, and came here to learn and help others learn."

21

Ainslee laid across the bed, asleep, when William returned back to their residence. It looked like she had made an attempt to stay awake and wait for him, but had given in to the late hour and her exhaustion. Neither surprised William. It sounded like she had had a pretty exhilarating day walking around the city, he was sure that had exhausted her. His night out had exhausted him.

He studied the bed for a moment, and considered waking her up or trying to move her over himself, to make some room. She looked so serene and almost angel-like sleeping there, he couldn't bring himself to do either. Not to mention, William didn't see how he could move her without waking her, as he would have to pick her up. Instead, he surveyed the room for another area for him to lay down and get some sleep. There was a long chair, covered in what appeared to be red velvet, against the wall under the windows. It looked long enough for him to stretch out on. What he was questioning, though, was its width. If he laid on his side, it might work. If he rolled at all, he might wake up to a momentary weightless feeling before his body thudded to the floor. There was always the floor, but the tiles looked hard and cold. With all the blankets on the bed, under his wife, that was the least attractive of all options. So, the red chair it was.

To try to prevent rolling off the chair, William pressed his back against the back of the chair. That left only a few inches between his body and the edge of the seat. It was unsettling, but he was tired, and his eyelids were growing heavy. He wasn't in the mood to search for another location. His world was going dark as a delicate voice asked, "What are you doing? Get over here in bed."

With a groan, he lifted his head and opened his eyes. Ainslee was sitting up in bed and patting her hand on the side he slept on last night. His body was tired and settled, but the pain in his back from the lack of comfort in the chair spoke louder. She pulled the covers back to welcome him to bed, and wrapped her arms around him as he laid down. The warm breath he felt on his neck, now, was more welcome than what he felt earlier.

"Late studying?", she whispered into his ear.

William yawned and said through a second yawn, "Training. Forty foot demon that looked like a bull running up and down the road. An old five foot tall man took care of it."

He heard her say, "What?", but after that his eyelids won and the room went dark.

23

The morning began the same way the previous morning had. Sister Francine knocked with a polite rap on their door. William heard it, but waited a moment before he stirred. His body argued with his brain about whether it was ready to wake up. The wait must have been longer than he thought, or that Ainslee would tolerate, as she got out of bed and proceeded to the door. When she opened it, the sister brought in the tray like she had yesterday, but there was a difference. Her eyes weren't down at the floor like before. Instead, they were locked on the location William's demonic visitor stood.

As Ainslee inspected the tray, she saw William was now sitting up in the bed. "Good morning, sleepyhead," she said.

"Morning," he said, as he swung his legs out of the bed and headed to the bath.

"So, any more wild dreams last night?", she asked.

"No," he responded. He must have been exhausted, as he hadn't dreamt at all, or he didn't remember any that he had. It was a curious question, though. "What do you mean?"

"You mentioned a forty foot bull when I woke you to come to bed."

William remembered saying something about it before he fell asleep, but couldn't remember how much he had told her. It was easy for him to see how someone who wasn't there, and didn't have all the other experiences he has had throughout his life, could see that as a wild dream. There was a brief thought in his head to tell her it was just a dream and protect her from any fear that might come from knowing demons like that really existed, but that thought lasted only a few seconds. She was his wife, and part of his life now. There was no shielding her from that. "Oh, that wasn't a dream. That was real," he said.

A loud clang echoed from the other room.

"You okay?", he asked as he poked his head through the door into the main room. Being okay was a relative state. Ainslee was alive and uninjured, sitting there at the table, with a shattered coffee cup on the floor and her face frozen with her mouth and eyes wide open, but her world would never be the same.

"This is not a joke?", she asked. A hint of a quiver in her voice.

"This is not a joke. It was real. Cristobal took me out with a group of others to handle a demon called Morax," said William. He used a white linen to dry the water he had splashed on his face. He intended to take a bath, but needed to handle this first. Ignoring the cup on the floor for the moment, he spun the other chair around and sat on it backwards, facing her. His arms were crossed along the top of the chair. "Ainslee, I know this all seems and sounds crazy, but this is all true. It is not a trick. There is more to the world than you know. I have known since I was very young."

"But this?", she interrupted. "You see monsters, too?"

"Well, to be honest, from what I understand, you could see them, too."

That statement slapped her straight back in the chair. Her quick movement made the chair skip backwards. One of its legs hit a portion of the cup and sent it skidding across the floor like a demonic top.

"Cristobal told me demons appear to the living in many forms. Sometimes they appear like what we saw last night. Sometimes as a person. Every time it is for the same purpose, though. They want to manipulate you. They will make promises to make you follow them willingly, and if that doesn't work, they will possess your soul... or something like that. I am still learning."

Before William had headed inside the night before, Cristobal had explained that that was what had happened to his wife, and why she had been acting like she was. When the demon promised to save her son in return for her help, it had expected her to do exactly as it said. She had refused him that last night, so it took possession of her soul and used her body as a vessel to carry out his doings. The concept of possession was one William was not that familiar with, but he had heard Father Henry mention it during some of his sermons. The facts Cristobal shared scared him far more than any fire and brimstone point Father Henry had been attempting. Chills rolled through his body as he heard stories about people mumbling in multiple voices, in all different languages, at the same time, scratches that appeared in victims from inside out, body parts contorting to the point of snapping bones, and strange fluids dripping from every orifice in the body. As shocking as those stories were, the ones about the exorcisms Cristobal had witnessed made him want to swim all the way back to his simple life in St. Margaret's Hope, and never look back. William had to ask if he would be expected to do exorcisms. Cristobal reassured him that he wouldn't, or at least not that type. That in a way what he was doing with the spirits was an exorcism, but he wouldn't be asked to perform a real one, those were reserved for trained priests only.

"How many have you seen?"

"Two, counting last night," William answered, not pausing long enough for her to say anything else before he added, "but those are just the ones I know of. Like I said, they could take any form."

Several deep sighs escaped Ainslee as William got up and picked up the jagged pieces of the broken porcelain coffee cup. There was a small puddle of coffee just beneath the table. William was on his way to retrieve the same towel he had used to dry off his face when she sighed again and asked, "So I could be a demon?"

To say that was not the next comment he was expecting from his wife would be the understatement of the year. His back was to her when she said it, but he stopped and spun around. There she sat, on the chair, with a pool of brown coffee underneath her, and that same mischievous smile on her face that he saw that day in the woods when they were younger. "You aren't taking this seriously, are you?"

"I am," she said. A crooked smile adorned her face.

"You know they can kill you if they want," William said.

The cute crooked smile on Ainslee's face melted away into one of worry and dread. Her head dropped and she looked around the room. The air had been knocked out of her attempt to bring levity to their morning, and now she took two deep breaths to regain it.

"It's true, they can hurt or kill you, but you need to know, you are in no more danger from them now than you were before. The only difference is you know about it."

"Okay," she said, and then she said it again, "Okay." The second one softer than the first. Her eyes continued to wander around the room.

He attempted to reassure her, "Trust me, you are in no more danger than you were before. Don't worry about it."

She muttered "Okay" two more times.

He meant what he said. There was no point in her worrying about any of this. She was just as likely to encounter a demon before as she is now. In fact, the way he thought about it, she was better off knowing about them. She is now aware that they exist, and can be on the alert when one tries to manipulate her. William hoped in time she might look at it this way, along with the rest of what they would both learn about this new life. What he was sure of was, he didn't like seeing his wife so full of woe, especially not about something she had no control over.

She had just picked up the second coffee cup from the tray and started to lift it toward her mouth when William said, "I am serious. The ghosts I used to see around you back home were probably more dangerous."

The cup fell a few inches back to the table with a thud, and sloshed several drops of coffee onto the table. This time, the impact was not hard enough to crack or shatter the cup. Her face shot toward her husband, who was walking back with a towel in his hand and a wry smile on his face.

24

Wake up, head to the great library, read and study with Cristobal for 9 or 10 hours, and then return to his residence. That was the pattern William fell into for the next several days. Twice there was the extra treat of spending the last waning hours of sunlight walking around the surrounding streets and shops with his wife. They walked hand in hand through the streets and took in the sights. To two people from a sleepy farming and fishing town, Vatican City, and the surrounding city of Rome, was something neither had ever imagined existed. Their ever-present chaperone, Sister Francine, acted as a tour guide.

On the last day of their second week, she asked each of them if they wanted to walk a little further, there was something she thought they would really want to see. It was only late afternoon, with plenty of light left in the day, but that didn't factor into their decision much. The level of enthusiasm Sister Francine showed, the first sign of any emotion William had seen from her, was what convinced them. They walked southwest, away from the Vatican and out of Vatican City. She and Ainslee had gone as far as the Tiber River a few times, but never across. This time, the three of them walked across the river and continued down the home and shop-lined street.

People, friendly people, were all over the place, going about their business. Some alone, some in couples, and others as families with children. All exchanged a pleasant greeting with one another as they passed, even with Ainslee and William, people they had never met. They were strangers in a strange world, but they felt as welcome as if they had always been here. Soon they approached the Piazza del Campidoglio. Up the incline they walked and out into the Roman Forum. Sister Francine kept moving at a steady pace, but William and Ainslee fell behind. The sight of the old roman arches, pillars, and other ruins was distracting them from their walk. Their eyes gazed skyward, with their necks stretched to take in the view. They rejoined their guide at a magnificent stone archway that she told them was called the Arch of Titus.

William had seen old buildings before, even what some might call ruins, but nothing like this. Nothing over a thousand years old, and nothing so grand. "I want to thank you for taking us and showing us these wonders," he said to Sister Francine.

His statement elicited the giggle of a young girl from her. The reaction of the reserved nun confused him, or it did until she took both of them by the hand and walked them to the left, around the arch. Neither William nor Ainslee could open their eyes wide enough to take in what she had just shown them. It was enormous. The thought that man could build something so large was hard for either to fathom. Before they had a chance to ask what it was, she told them it was called "the Coliseum".

They made one trip around the structure as Sister Francine explained its history. The explanation, and the ensuing questions from both of her guests, continued all the way back to the Vatican, to their room, and even when she re-entered a short time later with their dinner. If they thought the world they'd known in their old life was small before, this made it seem minuscule.

After dinner, William had planned to take Ainslee out to the steps to enjoy the star-filled night Cristobal had shown him last week. It was a spot he had visited twice since, to ponder what he had learned, and his purpose there. Both were still hard for him to have a complete grasp of, but he was getting it. When he opened the door to walk her out, Cristobal was standing there, again with two monks holding lanterns, and another figure hidden in the darkness down the hall.

"Good evening, Ainslee. Do you mind if we borrow your husband tonight? We have some work to do."

"Of course not. More demon hunting?", she asked.

In the light cast by the lanterns, Ainslee could see the uncomfortable look upon the faces of the two monks. She looked at Cristobal, who looked at her with a stoic expression. In an attempt to recover, she asked, "Can I walk him out? We were on our way out to look at the stars."

Cristobal didn't say anything, he just smiled and bowed as she exited holding William's hand. Cardinal Depeche led the procession down the hallway, with the lantern-holding monks behind him. Ainslee, William, and Cristobal followed close behind. When they exited, the procession didn't stop. At the top of the stairs, Ainslee gave her husband a quick kiss and sat down. From there, she watched the group walk through and out of the plaza.

"So, I will ask the same question my wife did. Are we going after another demon?"

"Not tonight. Tonight, is an important night. You are to show us what you have learned," said Cristobal.

"So, I am facing it?", asked William. A sliver of trepidation set in at the thought of going to battle with a demon like he witnessed the other night.

Cristobal laughed and said, "No, not a demon. This is just a run-of-the-mill spirit." With a slap on his back he added, "You shouldn't have any trouble with this. Just go with what you have learned."

The group walked, and walked, and walked. William's legs were still feeling the long walk to and from the Coliseum. The extra miles were adding to the muscle soreness he felt, the cold brisk night wasn't helping things much either.

Deep into the night, along a tree-lined road that headed out of Rome, the group paused at a cross-street while Cardinal Depeche studied their surroundings. In front of them was a dense grove of trees. To either side were roads that lead out, away from the city, with sparse buildings positioned on what looked like farms under the pale light of the moon. The gas lamps that lit the city were non-existent here. Darkness enveloped everything that wasn't in the glow of the light from either of the two lanterns the monks carried, or the light from the full moon high above them. He acted like he was searching for a landmark to determine which road to take, but that wasn't it. William knew it, but he wasn't sure who else did either. The cold sweat and row of pin pricks on the back of his neck were his tell-tale signs that their destination was close.

A hand emerged from under the red robe and waved for someone to walk forward. Neither of the two monks moved, but Cristobal took a single step forward and nudged William to move, as well. They joined Cardinal Depeche at the front, Cristobal stayed just a step or two behind, where he could serve as a translator. Fear of what was out there didn't consume William, nor should it. He couldn't remember the last time a spirit had made him afraid, but this was different. Others were watching, judging, what he did. That terrified him.

"William, He wants you to take the lead," said Cristobal.

"And do what?" William looked back at Cristobal with his eyebrows raised.

He waved William forward and said, "Show us what you've learned." Cardinal Depeche said a phrase in Italian. Cristobal translated, "Save the Spirit." He waved him forward again, and said, "Go on."

William took a few tentative steps off the road; in the direction he knew the spirit was. The chills that radiated down his body told him it wasn't too far away, and he was right. The dense forest of majestic Mediterranean cypress trees blocked the light of the full moon, casting the group in an eerie cocoon of darkness. Overhead, the treetops swayed, and the leaves chattered in the breeze, robbing them of any sense of calm and silence. The forest floor was barren, robbed of life-giving sunlight. This allowed William to move among the trunks unimpeded. The party that followed close behind weren't impeded either. They stayed just a few feet behind him at all times. William could feel the four sets of eyes on him from behind, and the spirit that grew closer ahead of him, with every step.

The towering cypress trees gave way to a grove of gnarled cork oak. The moonlight played in between their large, twisted, and distorted branches. The movement of the branches in the wind brought them and their shadows to life. Like a hideous beast living in hiding behind the cypress. William couldn't take his eyes off the shadows. The chill deepened inside him and a great weight landed on his shoulders. With each step, it became heavier and heavier. He felt his back and legs bending under the great force but, like Atlas, he straightened and pushed that force up, and steadied himself to support the weight of the world on his frame.

In the distance, among the old cork oaks, the flickering form came into view. The form was that of an older man. His black coat, and white shirt with ruffled cuffs, looked pristine. If it weren't for the blue flickering of the form, and the hollow eyes, one might think this were an Italian gentleman, out for an evening stroll in the light of a full moon. Make that an evening float. His legs moved as if he were walking, but they were three feet above the ground as he circled around and around the same tree.

William approached him, but he paid no attention as he circled around the tree again. Over the last three days Cristobal and William had talked about this very moment a great many times. Not the test, or whatever this was, but the moment when he would stand in front of a spirit and try to help it find its way. Based on his teachings, William had thought there would be more to it. With all the focus on why spirits remain connected to the world of the living, he expected to have to resolve or remove that connection to free them, but that was not the case. Cristobal had said they were not connected, so much as stuck, and needed encouragement to move on. During their lessons William was surprised, and disappointed, to learn there was not just one way to provide that. In fact, there are many ways, the challenge was knowing what was needed for each situation. He reminded William, no one said this would be easy, in fact, it was hard, but he was chosen to have this gift for a reason. William found it interesting no one had told him what that reason was.

Holding his hand up toward the spirit. Not being the most religious of people, William didn't have any bible verses memorized. William began, "O' heavenly Father. I request you give me the power to help this soul."

The spirit passed right by William and kept going around the tree.

He moved closer and began again, "God Almighty, help this lost soul find his way home."

Again, the spirit didn't look at him, didn't pause, and didn't stop.

Feeling a slight flush in his face more than the chills, he moved closer and put his hand up again. A strong and determined voice behind him shouted "Fermare! Fermare! Fermare!" before William was able to utter another world.

He looked around and saw Cardinal Depeche marching forward. The red-cloaked man passed by him and proceeded to a spot a few feet closer to the spirit than William had stood. He stood there with his hands crossed in front of him at his waist. No hand held up toward the spirit, or anything. In an even tone of voice, he said, "Devo confrontarti con una giornata estiva? Sei più adorabile e più temperato. I venti forti agitano le care gemme di maggio, E la locazione estiva ha un appuntamento troppo breve."

The spirit stopped in its tracks and hovered there. It turned ever so slightly in the direction of the cardinal. Without another word, the cardinal turned and walked back toward William. He stopped and tapped him dead center in his chest and said, "From here." He tapped William on the chest a final time before he walked back to join the others.

"What did he say?", asked William as he turned back toward Cristobal for guidance.

"From here."

"No. Not that. What did he say to make it stop?"

Cristobal chuckled before responding, " Shall I compare thee to a summer's day? Thou art more lovely and more temperate. Rough winds do shake the darling buds of May. And summer's lease hath all too short a date. It's Shakespeare's Sonnet #18."

If the feeling of embarrassment wasn't enough before, it was boiling over now. The cardinal had upstaged him by reading a poem. William knew it could have been worse, he could have just read his favorite recipe.

"William. Remember what we have talked about. Remember the other night in the road, and what we talked about then."

He turned back to the spirit and taking Cristobal's reminder to heart, he focused. Not on the words he would say, not on any thought of projecting something through his hand, but on believing. Believing he was there to help this soul. Believing this soul was being tormented here, and need to be freed to ascend to heaven. Believing he would be easing someone's pain. As he thought about this and reaffirmed his belief, the ground around him began to glow. The glow was not large, just a small circle, as if William were holding a single candle. At the same time, the spirit moved closer to him and stopped in front of him.

The more he believed, the wider the glow grew along the ground around him. What happened next was beyond anything William could have expected. The glow contacted the ground below the spirit, and the blue flickering haze stopped and disappeared. The spirit was still there, but it was different now. It was alive. The blue haze disappeared, leaving a person of pink and white flesh. There was even a sparkle in his brown eyes, and the light breeze blew his mane of jet-black hair. It still hovered above the ground, but the eerie figure was almost, more than almost, human.

A peaceful calm inside William accompanied the transformation. The chill he felt when spirits were around was gone and replaced by a warm feeling. A feeling of purpose. Without even thinking about it, William whispered, "You are free."

The spirit nodded and faded away into nothingness. William turned back to the group, with the hope of seeing approving and pleased looks. The ones he saw were not ones he would describe like that, though. Shocked looks were plastered across both the cardinal and Cristobal's faces. Even the two monks had broken decorum and pushed their hoods off of their heads, and shared the same expression.

25

The party returned back to the Vatican in silence. William's legs weren't silent. The euphoria he felt from his moment of success was overshadowed by the protest of his legs. Their trek to the Coliseum earlier in the day, and now this adventure at night, had taken their toll. Even the short but wide steps up the front of the Vatican were a strain for his tired muscles. He looked forward to lying down in his bed and getting some rest as they crossed through the golden doors, but that rest would have to wait. The glowing orbs of light produced by the two lanterns did not follow the sparsely lit hallway toward his residence. They didn't even turn in that direction. Instead, they continued to walk forward, through the great entryway and into a different room. William and Cristobal followed.

The sight of Cardinal Depeche descending down some stairs produced a groan inside William's mind, but he made sure to not vocalize it. He followed, legs aching with each step, down the spiral staircase. The flicker of the lanterns played against the stone block walls of the narrow passage. A cool, damp, musky air greeted the group at the bottom. The finished walls, paintings, and marble floors that decorated the floors above were nonexistent here. Replaced by stacked stone block walls and simple cobblestoned floors. Some had a green and grey moss growing on them. The passageway was as narrow as the stairs, with a few plain wooden doors with large black hinges, much like William was used to back home.

Cristobal pressed himself against the walls and slid past the two monks. There was an eagerness and urgency to his movements, and a sternness to his expression. Once he reached the front, William heard the murmur of a conversation between Cristobal and Cardinal Depeche. He couldn't hear any specific words, not that it would matter, as it was probably in Italian, but could tell one side of it was heated. The hand gestures made by Cristobal were rather animated, as was the rest of his body movements as he talked. In contrast, the Cardinal stayed a picture of calm and tranquility, as he continued to walk down the passage.

The discussion continued as the group stopped in front of one of the plain wooden doors. Cardinal Depeche turned to a large iron handle, and the clunk of the lock opening echoed up and down the passageway like a rumble of thunder. He entered the room, as did Cristobal, but both monks did not. They stepped to either side of the door, placed the lanterns they held down on the cobblestone floor, knelt, and bowed their heads. Each began praying, over and over. William watched the doorway for either Cristobal or the cardinal to return, but they didn't. Only a flicker from the lighting of a lantern emerged through the door.

"William!", commanded Cristobal from inside the room.

William entered. It was a small room, constructed with the same block walls and cobblestone floors as the passage. Wooden tables lined each wall. A cloth covered each of the tables, but they didn't lay flat. There were objects underneath the cloths. It was obvious to William the objects were placed with care, the same amount of empty space between each. It was as if they were placed on display, but that didn't make a lot of sense to him, since they were hidden from sight.

Cardinal Depeche and Cristobal were still amidst their conversation at the table opposite of where William stood. From there he could tell the cloth had been raised, exposing one of the items, but his view of the item was obscured by the cardinal. He wasn't sure if it was something that was said, or the item itself, that caused the most vehement protest by Cristobal yet. Whatever was the cause, the Cardinal put it down with a single hand gesture, and a look William could not see.

He turned to William and motioned for him to join them at the table. When he walked forward, he saw an item that was uncovered on the table. It was a simple wooden cross. It looked old, and was chipped on some of the edges. The cardinal took William's right hand and pressed it down on the cross. He was firm with the pressure as he pushed his hand on to the object.

"William," Cristobal said, then he paused. His eyes glanced around the room and he swallowed hard. An awkward silence filled the room. The cardinal nodded to him, but Cristobal didn't say or do anything. His discomfort with what he was being asked to do was almost palpable. The cardinal again gestured toward him, this time with a bit of emotion.

"Fine. Fine," he said and then continued, "William, your hand is on a cross made from wood taken from the cross Christ himself was crucified on. It was retrieved and returned to Pope Urban II during the first crusade. The wood, stained with the blood of our lord and savior, was carefully pulled apart and then crafted into a series of crosses. One is in the possession of our Holy Father, and one is in possession of the priest assigned to each of the known spiritual centers around the world. It is believed to help focus your abilities when dealing with both spirits and demons of the highest abilities. Cardinal Depeche is assigning you this cross to assist you in your duties. What you showed tonight is an ability beyond what we expected. We thought you were what we call a sensitive. One that can sense and interact with the spiritual world, but you go far beyond that. You are what we call a keeper, the first non-priest keeper we have ever met. A keeper is responsible for keeping the world of the living safe from spirits and demons."

William's mind stopped hearing what was said after he was told his hand was pressed against a cross made of wood from the crucifix of Christ. When that realization hit him, he attempted to pull his hand back, but the cardinal's grip was firm and steadfast. He didn't feel worthy of touching it. This was one of the most religious items in the world, and he was just a simple farmer. Then the irony hit him. Jesus Christ is called a prince, but in his mortal life he was not. He was a common carpenter, who made tools for simple farmers, much like William.

Cardinal Depeche released William's hand, which recoiled a few inches above the cross. He motioned with his hands for him to pick up the cross. William's hands shook as he did so. At first glance, it was a simple aged wooden cross, but at a closer look it was something more, much more. It was constructed of four distinct pieces, morticed together in the center. The chips he saw on the edges were not from damage, but were the imperfect cuts of the axes and blades that had shaped the original cross Christ was mounted on. Each of the four pieces of wood used contained spots that were darker than the others, it wasn't just darker aged wood, they were stained with something, something red, the blood of Christ.

"William," Cristobal pleaded as he walked closer to him. "You can refuse this assignment. When we talked about demons, I told you only priests challenge them. It is extremely dangerous, and should only be attempted by the most faithful and pious among us. I must admit to you openly, I am against this. I agree you have a gift, a great gift, and you can use it to be a sensitive, but a priest who is a keeper should be assigned with you. That is how it is done."

A hand emerged from under the red robe of the cardinal and he motioned for William to bend down to him. Instead, William knelt down on one knee, bringing him face to face with him. The weathered and wrinkled face of the cardinal took on a fatherly look. His eyes kind and calm as he said in English, through his thick accent, "You are the one. The one who can do this." Before William could respond or ask a question, the cardinal leaned forward and kissed him on the forehead, and then used the thumb of his left hand to draw a cross on the spot he kissed. Then the man walked out of the room, leaving him standing there with Cristobal.

"And if I choose to do this?", asked William, not that he had chosen one way or the other. He didn't know how to decide on something like this. It was not your typical, 'What do you want for breakfast?' or 'In which plot does you plant what this season'? Which were some of the more difficult decisions he had made so far in his life. The only one more difficult had been to follow Bishop Emmanuel this far. He did so because he wanted an adventure, and an adventure he had found.

"Then I will train you, but you will have to accept a life more challenging than you could ever imagine."

26

"That is what?", exclaimed Ainslee as she retreated back to their bed. On their table sat a simple wooden cross, alongside a brown leather-bound book. When he explained what the cross was, what color existed in her fair complexion drained out of her face, her hand sprang up to her mouth, and she stumbled backwards to the bed.

"The wood is from the cross Christ was crucified on," explained William, for a second time now.

"Why... Why? Did they give that to you?", she asked. Her speech stuttering every syllable as she fanned herself with both hands.

William explained to her what Cristobal and Cardinal Depeche told him. He knew she would have questions when he completed the recollection. To try to head off any questions of the "This is so hard to believe" variety, he retold her about the night he watched Cardinal Depeche battle Morax. On the way back to his residence, Cristobal had told him that the relic the cardinal possessed was a piece of cloth from the burial shroud that was draped over Christ in his tomb. It was only a few inches square, but its ability to focus the cardinal's capability was not limited by its physical size. Something William could attest to from what he saw that night. The creature they'd fought was over forty feet tall, yet that small piece of cloth had brought it howling to its knees.

"Come on over. This and the leather-bound book will be part of our lives. Don't be scared of them." William stood over the table and motioned for her to join him again, but she was hesitant. He motioned again and she got up off the bed and took several tentative steps with her lower body, toward the table. Ainslee's upper body seemed less eager to approach the objects. It leaned back about as far as it could, without causing her body to fall backward. Balls of fabric from the skirt of her simple light blue dress her and Sister Francine had bought together the day earlier were kneaded by each fist.

At the table, William picked up the cross and attempted to hand it to her, but she again recoiled. He took her hand, forcing it to release the fabric of her skirt, and placed it on it. He knew darn well what she was going through. It was the same thoughts he had experienced mere moments ago. His hand was forced on the cross, like hers was now. Thoughts flooded into his head of not being worthy of touching something so sacred. Expectations of some great feeling that would pulse through him, or an explosion of light that would radiate from it as if it were the sun high in the sky on a summer day, with a chorus of angels singing in unison but only in his head. What his hand felt was a simple wooden cross. It was nothing to be scared of. That is what he kept telling himself. The object was just an object, but its sanctified beginnings reflected the responsibility that was bestowed upon him, and that was what he was afraid of.

The resistance in her arm dissipated the longer he held her hand on it. Before long he was able to remove his hand and, she kept her hand on it before eventually picking it up and studying it. The delicate fingers of her right hand held it firmly, while the fingers of her left hand caressed every edge and surface. The fear that was on her face before had been replaced with the curiosity of a young child exploring the outside world for the first time.

"What are these darker stains?", she asked, as she attempted to smell the odor of the wood.

William considered telling her what it was right away, but his mind played the image of her dropping the cross, sending it crashing to the floor in a heap of splinters. To avoid such a disaster, he suggested, "Why don't you put it on the table before I tell you?"

The curiosity that was there was replaced by a set of perplexed eyebrows. He knew the pouty look would follow, it was predictable, and how she got her way so often.

"Ainslee, put it down and I will tell you," William suggested again. This time his voice held an air of seriousness.

The suggestion worked this time. She placed the cross down on the table, next to a simple brown leather-bound book. William also managed to head off the pouty look, but the one that replaced it bothered him more so. The dropped shoulders and eyes reminded him of how she would look when her father scolded her. A look he never wanted to be the cause of, and from this day forward he swore to himself he would never do so again. The only way he could correct it was to answer her question, so she could realize, herself, why he wanted her to put it down first.

"Those stains are the blood of Christ."

He was right to have had her put it down before he told her. Upon hearing what it was, she fell to the floor with a thud. She landed on her butt and sat there, with both arms outstretched. A look that was a mixture of fear and surprise filled her eyes as they scanned back and forth, from one hand to the other. Her lips mumbled, "I touched the blood of Christ."

"Yes, you did," William said as he extended a hand toward his bride, to help her up. No attempt was made on her end to take his hand, so William reached down and attempted to grab her right hand. It moved away from him before he was able to grasp it. The hand was spread wide, and held up toward her husband, to show him what was on it. In truth, there wasn't anything on it. It was as clean as could be. The stains were part of the wood, and didn't bleed off on your skin.

"There is nothing on your hand. Come on. Let's get you up," he said as he made another attempt to grab her hand. She avoided him again, but this time her husband outsmarted her and grabbed her left hand, pulling her to her feet. Once up, he pulled her close, but her eyes stayed on the table.

"What is the book? Is that his journal?"

"No, it's my journal, and it's empty."

27

After the excitement of the new members of their family, both William and Ainslee gave in to the late hour of the night and fell asleep. Every night William fell asleep gazing at his wife, but not tonight. His eyes stared across the room at an object that sat flat on the table. Inside, he couldn't shake the expectations his mind imagined. So much mysticism surrounded what it was, how could it just sit there and not emit a glow in the darkness of the room? Shouldn't it hum, make some noise, or levitate above the ground like Jesus when he walked on the water in the book of Matthew? The fact was, it didn't. It gave no sign outwardly that it was special, but then again, neither did William. What was there was a strong belief. Something he reminded himself of as his vision narrowed and his nose smelled the last wafts of the remnants of the jasmine bath Ainslee had taken just before bed. What William didn't know was, his wife, who usually looked at him until she fell asleep, was looking across the room at the same object he was, with very similar thoughts, until exhaustion took her under.

The thoughts that had consumed William's mind before he fell asleep dominated his dreams. Fields of flowers, under beautiful blue skies, that started light blue at the horizon and grew to a deep royal blue the higher you went up, provided him and Ainslee a paradise to explore. The warm glow of sunlight basked him in life-giving energy, while a babbling brook serenaded them in a relaxing chorus. Firmly in his hand was the cross. As he pointed it in a direction, it projected a white light so bright it was almost blinding. It did not burn or destroy anything it came in contact with, it purified them. The flowers were brighter and more fragrant. The sky more vivid.

They walked through the meadows toward the brook, the scent of each flower they passed was overwhelming to the senses. A horde of butterflies scattered as they walked through a grouping of white lilies that stood knee-high to each of them. On the other side of the lilies, they found themselves standing on the bank of the brook. It appeared shallow, very shallow. River rocks below the surface created a washboard current for as far as William could see. He took a step in, leading Ainslee with him. It was not cool as he expected. It was something he had never experienced before, it was warm. He found himself standing ankle-deep in warm water, and it was getting warmer, and deeper.

It reached his knees without him having to move an inch. Overhead, the skies clouded up as if a storm front was approaching, but instead of just turning dark, the sky had a red haze to it. "Red sky at night, sailor's delight, but red sky at morn, sailor's be warned," was a saying he remembered his uncle saying. The problem was, he didn't know whether this was morning or night. He didn't have time to worry about that now. The water reached his waist, and the temperature had become uncomfortable, sending his upper body into a flop sweat. Right before his eyes, the lilies that bordered the brook turned to dried stems and wilting petals. As he looked around at the changing scene around him, he realized Ainslee was gone. The last time he saw her was before the water had started to rise. Afraid she had disappeared below the water, he tried to turn and search for her, but his feet were locked in place in the creek bed.

The water bubbled around his body, and his skin sizzled as the water surrounded his chest. Breathing became labored and painful. His skin was scalded, and yellow pus-filled blisters covered every inch of its surface. The urge to scream was primal, instinctual, but he couldn't. Water surrounded William's throat, and the steam that rose from its surface robbed him of the necessary oxygen. All around him the sky began to bleed, from just above the horizon, down to the ground. First slight drips, and then gushing flows. When it reached the ground, it continued and raced toward him like a great tsunami of red. A ring of fire exploded in the sky over his head. Waves of fire rolled across the sky toward the blood running down the horizon. Where they met, the flame congealed into a red fluid and joined the flood of red blood rushing across the landscape. The top of his head baked, and his body boiled. Pain soared through his being, forcing his eyes closed.

When William next opened them, he was back in his residence, lying in their bed, but all was not well. The full-on body sweat might have hinted at a terrifying nightmare, but that didn't explain the river of flame that surged across the ceiling, the fingers of which turned into blood when it hit the wall. Red liquid flowed down the surface of every wall, into a foot or more of the substance already pooled on the floor. Beside him, his wife laid silently, but her body cooked from the outside in. Her flesh grew taut and cracked, like the skin of a large sow on a flame pit. Singe marks covered her face. She did not scream. She did not move.

William tried to jump up and carry her to safety, but the bed linens trapped him where he was. Another pull, and he was jerked back the few inches they gave. An attempt to scream was met with nothing but silence escaping his open mouth, as a great force pulled him down deeper into the bed.

"Now, now, William. There is no reason to scream. You knew this was coming." The voice echoed from everywhere, and nowhere, all at once. It rattled the room and sent ripples running up the waterfall of blood flowing down the walls. Above him, the color of the flames changed from orange to yellow, and then the edges of a spot of white flame came into his view. It was a small circular spot, but grew by the moment. At the center sat a dark dot that grew in size within the circle of white flames. The dot took on a shape, an oval. No that wasn't it. It was a head, and not just any head. A head with a face, with horns sticking out from each side.

The head descended to just above William, along with its upper body, which hung out of the circle of white flames. "Hi, William," said the face.

William knew this head, this face, and the voice that echoed. This would now be its third visit.

"Leave her alone," William croaked. He intended to yell that demand, but the great force pressing him into the bed restricted his lungs' ability to take the gulp of air he needed.

"I gave you a choice. You should have taken it. It was a real peachy life."

It leaned over the top of Ainslee and grinned an evil grin. William tried again to break free, but the force pressed him back into the impression his body had made in the mattress. He struggled as a long and jagged claw descended past his head. A muscular arm of molten material connected it to the creature's right shoulder socket. The creature turned to look at William, with the same evil grin, as the claw drew a line down Ainslee. A white haze shined up from the line as her skin peeled back to either side. It turned its attentions back to her as it started to dissect her inch by inch.

William jerked his body wildly to either side, in a move that resembled a turtle having a convulsion while it tried to flip itself back over on its feet. His arms flung wildly at first, gaining just inches, but worked their way free, while the creature's attentions were on his wife. Faced with the choice of reaching over and trying to stop whatever was happening to her, if he even knew how, and going for help, in a sheer moment of panic he chose the latter. He was sure either Cristobal or the cardinal would know what to do. With his arms free, he pried himself off the bed and fell to the floor. The sound of his body slamming on the solid floor got both his and the creature's attention. A question rushed into William's head. "How do you slam in several feet of pooled blood?"

A wiggle of his toes confirmed the answer. There was no blood. None of this was real. He hoped what was happening to Ainslee wasn't either. There was only one way to find out, he had to stop and dismiss this creature, who Cristobal had told him was one of Morax's agents. William stood up, confident and strong. His body screamed in defiance and his eyes searched for the table. The creature was alarmed by these events, and thrust its hand into what was left of Ainslee's body. It cackled a thunderous laugh that pushed William back to the ground but, once again, he didn't splash down, he crashed on the floor. Even falling backward to the floor, his eyes stayed fixed on the table.

The creature spun around and followed William's focus to the table. It hovered above the bed, frozen in place. From his vantage point, William thought he could detect a slight wrinkle of its brow, and downturn of its lips. It was fear, and he had every intention of using it.

William leapt to his feet and ran to the table. The creature was transfixed by the objects laying on the table, and never saw him approach. It never saw his hand reach into its view and grab the cross. It never saw him thrust the cross up into it. His heart was full of the belief that the object, and his faith, would send that creature back where it belonged.

In that instant, the sea of blood on the floor disappeared, and the fire above his head receded back into the circle of white flame. The creature pulled back up into the circle and, in a flash, both were gone, leaving the room bathed in the darkness of night. The only sounds were the crickets outside the open window, and the deep and restful breathing of his asleep in bed.

He watched her laying there, peaceful, as his mind tried to remove the images it had been presented just moments ago. The thought that what he had seen could have happened, shook him to his core. His thoughts went back to Cristobal's story about his own wife. Over and over, William wondered if that could happen to Ainslee. His decision to do this was putting her in harm's way, and he felt both guilty and responsible for that. She would be safe, back at home in St. Margaret's Hope, if he hadn't brought her here with him, and exposed her to these dangers. The truth was, he wasn't aware of these dangers then, but that counterargument did little to quell the fear he felt, or the gnawing feeling in his gut that he needed to send her home.

A scream, followed by a second, and more harrowing one, interrupted the internal debate waging inside William. There was no question whether this scream was real or not. The second scream woke Ainslee up with a startle. "What was…" Her question was cut off by a third scream, and the sound of other voices yelling. Neither of them could understand what was being said, but the tone contained fear and violence. Before the fourth scream had completed its course down the hall, William had raced out the door, cross in hand, his footfalls echoing in the cavernous hallway along with the others that also raced toward the scream.

28

Another scream ravaged the darkness of the hallway. This scream was different than the others. It was most definitely not human. The sound was full of pain, sorrow, remorse, and hatred: pure unrestrained hatred. Following that were the exclamations of several men, in Italian, but there was one word William could recognize as clear as anything, "No!"

Behind William, other footsteps raced down the hall. He didn't know who it was, nor was he interested in turning around to find out. The source of the screams were his focus. If others were on their way to help, all the better, but not his concern. The darkness in the hallway cast a layer of confusion on where the screams were coming from. All William could do was follow his ears, but the cavernous size of the hallway masked the source, in the endless echoes of screams and cries.

A cloud of uncertainty overcame William at an intersection of corridors. Standing in the middle, the echoes seemed to emerge out of the darkness of each. The footsteps that had trailed him down the hallway caught up as he danced between the decision of continuing straight, or taking either the hallway to the right or the one to the left.

"Which way?" asked Cristobal, who had joined William in the center, just as confused as to where the source of the screams was coming from.

"I don't know."

Both men took steps down each hallway, listening, but the echoes continued to play tricks with them. As the seconds ticked by, William felt the muscles in his body tense up. He stretched his fingers and then clenched them in a fist, before stretching them again. His weight bounced back and forth on his legs as he moved to check each of the hallways for the source of the sound. Behind him, Cristobal was checking the opposite side for the source, and let out a guttural groan of frustration. Then it hit William.

He took one step further down the hall, and on the back of his neck there was a single cold prick of a pin. Another step, and several more prickles were followed by an outbreak of gooseflesh across his neck and down his back. With one more step, he knew for sure, especially when the familiar suffocating weight settled upon his shoulders.

"This way," he said, adding to the echo, and then sprinted down the hallway. Another set of footsteps followed close behind him. They were both still searching in the darkness for a destination they did not know, nor did they know what they would find once they'd reached the source of the screams. The weight pressing down on William, and the cold he felt in his core, told him they were getting close, but he neither needed nor wanted those signs. The bloodcurdling screams and cries were getting louder, and they were also getting clearer. He and Cristobal could now hear two distinct voices behind the screams. One was not human, something they already knew. The other was a voice they both recognized, Cardinal Depeche.

Cristobal sprinted past William, taking the lead down the hall and around the corner. Not knowing where the cardinal's room was, William was content with following. When he rounded the corner, there was no question of which door it was. Both men stumbled to a stop in front of the third door down on the right. An eerie red hue glowed through the gaps along all four sides of the door, and a scorching heat radiated outward.

"Fire!" screamed Cristobal, as he reached for the door.

Before his hand touched the handle, William grabbed his wrist and yanked it back. Cristobal responded with a look of shock, but William maintained his grip on his wrist and shook his head. The screams continued behind the door. The red glow intensified along with the inhuman scream full of hatred. Cristobal's head turned slowly from William's face toward the door. His eyes opened wide as the realization of what was behind the door hit him. William had known for several moments now.

Cristobal backed away from the door. His body trembled in fear. He was not alone. William felt it, too, along with all the other sensations that used to drive great fear in him, now he was used to them. The fear was palpable, and every scream allowed more of it to ooze out the door and attach itself to them, like a great parasite that fed on them and grew deep inside, until it was able to control them. Unless they took control of it first. That is what William did. He stepped forward and, with the crucifix clearly in his left hand, he reached with his right and opened the door.

A flash of flame threw both men against the opposite wall. The impact took William's breath away for a second. He rolled back over and looked toward the doorway. The large wooden door was now lying on the floor, several feet from William and Cristobal. Through the doorway, he could see the room engulfed in flames. They roiled up each wall, and across the ceiling. The screams continued, and sent ripples across the sea of fire.

William pushed himself back to his feet and walked through the doorway with his left hand out in front of him, to ensure the crucifix entered the room first. The heat was overwhelming, but he still felt the cold pinpricks from the back of his neck to the bottom of his spine. He looked around and saw no sign of the cardinal, but his scream continued, as did the other scream, the non-human scream.

The floor was clear of any fire, which allowed William to move inward freely. His eyes traced the fire from the bottom of the wall, up to the ceiling, and across. When he reached the image, he knelt down. Cardinal Depeche's body was suspended from the ceiling. Circulating bindings of flame were wrapped around both his arms and legs, as well as his neck. His screams were cut short by fingers of flame that reached over and shoved themselves through his open mouth, stifling the sound. When the fingers retreated from his mouth, his scream started again, and was allowed to persist for only a few moments. The fingers of flame cut them off again.

Movement to the right caught William's eye. He turned and saw one of the two monks, restrained by similar bindings of flame. His skin smoldered where it contacted the bindings, and produced billows of dark grey smoke. A quick search around the room found the second monk, restrained like the others, but the heat of his bindings had already reduced his body to a smoking skeleton.

Neither of the images frightened William as much as the deep snort that rumbled above his head. Full body trembles shook his vision as he looked up. A large hump circled the cardinal in the flames, as the whole mass pulsated up and down like a heartbeat. Large puffs of smoke bubbled from the hump with each snort.

He looked back. Cristobal stood in the open doorway, and crossed himself. Sheer terror dripped from his body. His body fell rigidly to his knees, like a plank of wood falling on one end. With his hands clasped in front of him, he started a prayer, but did not bow his head. With his eyes bulged out of their sockets, and his mouth gasping for air, he kept his head up, eyes fixated on the scene from the bowels of hell itself that was before him. His lips moved, but no sound escaped. The bulge slowed its rotation around the cardinal, but the snorts continued, more frequent than before, and more visceral.

It stopped, and the puffs of smoke spiraled toward the kneeling Cristobal. The fingers of flame flooded into the cardinal and silenced the start of another scream, sending the room into an eerie silence. Only snorts, and the low rumble of raspy breaths, interrupted the silence.

In and out.

In and out.

The breathing continued, slow and hollow, like wind flowing in and out of a large empty cave. William noticed with each breath in, the flames pulsated up, and then down with the exhale. William wondered if they were inside the beast, itself.

He wasn't given a lot of time to consider that, before horns broke through the bulge and the head of a bull charged at Cristobal. His friend was frozen in place, either by fear or by the power this demon had over him. William leapt in between the kneeling scholar and the head of the bull, a head he had seen before. With his left hand, he thrust the crucifix forward. The movements were strong and firm. As was his voice as he proclaimed, "Morax, you will stop."

The demon recoiled backward, and snorted a fire and smoke-filled breath that tousled William's hair, but he didn't move. Instead, he took a step forward and closed the gap. Morax roared with the voices of a thousand dead souls, but William didn't retreat, he took another step forward. Each step filled his heart with more belief, and a glow of white light began to radiate out along the floor. Morax dipped his head to look at the light and shook his head back and forth with an uncontrolled shudder. From inside the fire, ran the demon that had visited William three times over the past few weeks. It was smaller than he remembered as it ran along the neck of the great beast, but grew with each step. It leapt from its head through the air, toward William, but his resolve was solid, like a brick foundation a great house was built on. Cristobal and Cardinal Depeche had laid that foundation, and then given him the training, and the tools, to build upon it. This was a great test, like the arrival of the first hard storm a building will face. If built with the right tools and materials, he, like the building, would not crumble under the attack.

William held his position at first, and then stepped to the side and slashed at the demon with the cross. He commanded in a voice as strong as his body, "In the name of God, I condemn you." The force of the impact was not great, but the demon was sent across the room with a thud. Its body flailed on the floor, as it whined in a high pitched hum that pierced William's hearing. Its great claws dug at the floor to try to drag itself away from the fire. A hint of blue smoke rose above it. At first it was a light haze of blue, but grew denser, into a dark grey-blue. The piercing hum ceased and the flames that danced along its body dissipated, leaving a black form on the floor that collapsed into a pile of dust.

The fire that rolled up the walls receded up to the ceiling. On one side of the room, the scorched body of one of the monks collapsed to the floor. The skeletal remains of his counterpart crashed down on the other. William stepped forward again toward Morax, the light now covered the floor. The pulsating mass of fire above him skipped a beat. Its head jerked up and the flames that dripped from its horns lost their intensity.

"You're next," said William. The white light now halfway up the walls, on the way to the ceiling. Morax disappeared back into the bulge, and then up into the ocean of fire. Cardinal Depeche was released from his bonds and dropped to the floor, and the blaze above their heads began to swirl at a dizzying pace before disappearing with a roar that reverberated through every bone in William's body. The room returned to normal, no signs of anything having been burnt. William rushed over to the cardinal, who moaned and groaned in pain. Black and crisped skin circled his wrists, ankles, and neck. With the fall from the ceiling, William was sure one or more bones were broken as well. Cristobal was tending to the monk, who had suffered similar burns. There was nothing left of the other monk to help.

29

Exhausted, William dragged himself, body and soul, back down the dark hallway, leaving the madness of the last several minutes behind him. The room he left had no appearance that matched the horror of the scene he had walked in on. There were no scorch marks on the walls or ceiling from the pulsating flames; every piece of furniture was in its place. Even the bed was just slightly tousled, but that had happened when Cardinal Depeche jumped out to fight his visitor. What was damaged were the lives and faith of every person there. The smoking skeletal remains of a monk lay on the floor in a heap, resembling William's resolve. The monk's compatriot was alive, but in pain, with burns that still smoldered in his skin. Also, alive, but barely, was Cardinal Depeche. The burns around his neck, ankles, and wrists still smoldered deep inside his skin, and appeared to continue to spread up his arms and legs. William and Cristobal had attempted to provide aid, but neither could do anything more than try to keep both men calm, something they were having difficulty doing themselves.

A feeling of relief came over William as several members of the navy and gold-clad Vatican guard arrived. Both guards stood at the door for a few seconds, to take in the scene. Neither asked questions about what had happened before they took action. William figured this was something they may have been used to, or possibly instructed to not ask and just serve. One of the two guards rushed in to help, while the other rushed away. He helped stretch out Cardinal Depeche flat on the floor. The old man, diminutive to begin with, looked like a fragile creature who was clinging to life. His hands were balled up and held close to his body, shaking uncontrollably as he moaned, even though he was unconscious. The guard showed the cardinal the respect he deserved and neatly adjusted his robe around him. Next, the guard laid the monk out straight and flat on the floor. His body twitched as his fearful eyes looked up at the ceiling, in search of the beast that did this to them. He didn't utter a sound. The guard knelt between the two men and alternated his attention back and forth.

The second guard returned with two additional guards and a man wearing a dark robe with a long white beard. All four entered, but the guards remained standing at attention as the man in black knelt over the cardinal and then sprang up and ran around to the monk. While over each, he examined the burns, placed an ear to their chests, and held his hand under their noses. A phrase and question were spoken to the monk, but the monk didn't respond at first. The phrase was uttered again, and this time the man made eye contact with his patient. This must have been the first time he realized who it was, and he held his hand up to his face as the monk attempted to open his mouth to answer the questions.

He stood up and barked a command to the guard, in Italian. The four men paired off. Two grabbed the cardinal, one under his arms and one under his legs. He winced at their touch and his moans grew louder. The other two hoisted up the monk, who also winced, but remained silent. They rushed out the door and down the hall, throwing the room into silence, with the exception of the breathing of the two men left in the room, one of which was letting out a sigh of relief and the other was taking in fast, short, panicked breaths.

William turned to Cristobal, who was still sitting on his knees on the floor. His chin was pressed firmly into his chest, his hands sat on his legs, but they were not calm. Each finger dug into the fabric of his robe, released it, and then dug into it again, squeezing it as hard as his hands would allow. Something needed to be said between them, but William didn't know what that was, so he walked out, leaving the acrid smell of burnt flesh behind.

While William may have won, he felt physically and spiritually defeated. Not from any doubt in his abilities. When challenged, he put his skills to the test, and passed. At no time had he felt his faith wane or weaken. There was no pause before he took action. In fact, he felt surprised at how he had sprung into action, like a soldier on the battlefield of a war. In truth, this was a battle, one of hundreds, or even thousands, of battles in the war between good and evil. Since he had started his training, he wondered if it was possible for one side to win this war, and if it was, what would that look like? This was something deeper, and far beyond his ability to think about. What he did know was, he would not be the one to win the war, the best he could hope for was to string together enough victories in battle to keep from losing it. Then it hit him, why couldn't he win the war? Wasn't that what he was here to do? The weight of that realization collapsed down on him, already wearing on him, to further deflate his spirit. The gravity of that realization made every step down the hall, back to his residence, laborious.

His heart sank as the images of Ainslee being ripped apart from the inside flooded into his mind. Not a one of them was real. Nothing about what had happened to her was, but that didn't change how he felt in that moment. The only way he had survived was by realizing it wasn't real and dismissing it. Only then could he see through the illusion, and take control. He was able to push aside what he saw, freeing his mind and body. It removed the shackles of concern about what was happening around him and to someone he loved, from holding him back from taking care of what he needed to do. He now knows he was stupid and naïve. The scene he just left showed that people could be hurt, and even killed, when his adversary wanted to.

Why he hadn't realized that before, or comprehended the many times Cristobal had tried to tell him, he didn't know. What he did know was, taking on this responsibility put him, Ainslee, and any future family they could have, in direct danger. More so than just being brought into a world that was full of more dangers than he ever imagined, but they had a proverbial and literal target on their chests. Any conniving demon could use them to manipulate William, or another thought that had just hit him, as if he needed anything else that night. Their kids would not only be targets to manipulate William, they would be targets, themselves, to keep them from continuing this work on their own. Could he bring a family into this world with that threat? Could he live with himself if he did? Those were all questions that weighed on his soul, but there was one heavier than the rest, what had he got Ainslee into?

There was one thing clear to him, it was the thought that was foremost to him at that moment. He needed to talk to her and explain all this. When his mind should have been thinking about how, it had already jumped hours and days ahead, as he watched her sail away to return home to St. Margaret's Hope. The pain of losing her had already become a bad taste in his mouth that made him sick to his stomach. He saw no other outcome after what he needed to tell her. If only he had known, he wouldn't have dragged her in to all this. Bishop Emmanuel was really the person to blame. He knew all this and should have stopped them. William wondered if this was why he seemed to protest so hard in Father Henry's home that night. It probably was, and neither he, Father Henry, and definitely not Ainslee, had known enough to listen to him. He shook his head and muttered, "No. No," under a heavy breath. This was not their responsibility, it was his. The danger she was in was his fault, and his fault alone.

"Something troubling you, my son?", said a voice from the darkness. The voice had a soothing and calming tone to it.

William stopped and looked around through the shadows for the source of the voice. From what he could see, it was just, and only, him. "Who's there?", he asked.

Stepping from the darkness in front of him appeared a man dressed in a white robe, with a similarly white zucchetto on his head. Where had he come from? William was sure there was nothing there before, just dark empty space. Yet, as clear as the nose on his face, stood this man. This honorable man, with a sensitive and compassionate voice, and two kind eyes he could see from where he stood. The man took several unsteady steps that hinted at his age, which William guessed had to be almost 80. As he came closer, the creases of time were clearly visible on the man's face, but his eyes were still full of life.

"You look troubled," he said again.

"A tough night," responded William, as the man walked past.

A single hand rose up from the side of the man and motioned for him to follow. "Come, Let's talk."

At that moment, William recognized His Holiness and followed him. Unsure what the proper protocol was, he stayed behind him a step or two. There was something reverent about that moment. Walking through the halls of the Vatican with the Holy Father, himself, him, just a simple farmer from a small seaside village in Scotland.

"There are perfect days, and days that are less perfect. It is part of life. You know it is how you respond to them that shape who you are. I, myself, have been pushed to what I think is my breaking point, a challenge or problem too big for me. When that happens, I pray and search for guidance from my Lord. At times, he answers," his eyes and head tipped up toward the ceiling before he continued. "Sometimes he doesn't," he said with a laugh. "Oh, yes, even me. I don't take it personally. Instead, I take it as a message in its own way. It is his way of telling me to figure it out for myself, and you know what I do? I do. I walk these halls and pull in the inspiration from these very walls and take solace in the fact that they have seen challenges greater than the ones I have faced, and yet they have survived."

William realized he had followed him through the great hall, and both men were exiting through the golden doors, out into St. Peter's plaza. His Holiness paused at the top of the stairs. He held his hand out behind him. William took it and His Holiness squatted down and sat on the top step. There was a hidden strength in his old body that surprised William. Even though the arm shook slightly as he sat, William was not what helped him down, he was merely an anchor as he lowered himself to the step.

"And this, sitting at these doors, always helps me put my problems in perspective."

William remembered the night he and Cristobal had first sat on these stairs and looked up at the stars. Cristobal had described the same feeling from the scene, and assumed this was what His Holiness spoke about. "The night sky relaxes you, too."

"It does, but that is not it. It is the doors behind us. Those doors are always open for those with bigger problems than mine. Kind of puts everything in perspective, doesn't it?"

There was nothing William could say to that, so he just nodded, while imagining a line of people filing in slowly for guidance and help with their problems.

"You and I share a gift."

Again, William didn't say anything. This statement made more sense to him than the previous. He wondered if it was a requirement to be able to see ghosts and interact with that world.

"It is not what you think it is. Yes, I can see spirits and tend to their needs, but that is not what I speak of. We both share an ability to shoulder a great burden. My service comes with a great burden, but God gave me the ability to deal with the crushing weight of it. Your service comes with a similar burden, and," he paused, "God gave you the ability to handle that burden too. That is more important than seeing spirits and demons. Without it, you wouldn't be able to survive the other gift. You have to live life to the fullest, and trust in him. He would have not saddled you with this, and brought you to us, if he hadn't prepared you to handle it."

William found himself staring up at the stars while His Holiness spoke. Well, he wasn't looking at the stars, but past the stars. Through the vast darkness of space, in search of that place the human psyche believes and desires to be there. Up there is a golden throne, from which their creator looked over them and watched as HIS master plan proceeded, day after day, from the beginning of time until the end. It is not something the eyes can see, but the heart can. The spirit can. The emotional center of the person can, and it anchors them in beliefs such as, there is a plan for everyone, and this, too, must pass. There may be times in their lives that they lose faith in the plan or, even worse, question if there even is one, but they always return back to their beliefs, because even that will pass. They must trust in the plan, and this was the plan for him.

"You ok?"

William's body jerked back from its celestial search and landed within himself on the top step. Cristobal sat down beside him as his head whirled around, looking for His Holiness. He was nowhere in sight.

"William, you ok? You look like you have seen a ghost."

"Yea, ummm," his head turned around and searched the darkness inside the doorway for the frame of the old man, but there was nothing. "I didn't hear him leave."

"Who?", asked Cristobal.

"His Holiness, the pope."

"William! He is in France, and won't return for another few weeks."

William's body went rigid and he looked right at Cristobal. His eyes searched for any hint of a joke in his friend and teacher, but found nothing. "That is impossible. I was sitting right here next to him. We were talking."

Cristobal raised his chin up and looked out of the side of his eyes at William. A smirk was draped across his face. William just sat there, stone-faced. "Huh," Cristobal said as he turned his gaze to the plaza, "it would make sense."

"What would?", William asked.

"I am sure you wouldn't be surprised to know that spirits of past popes roam these halls. We believe their duty and service pull them back here after they pass. Not so much to help the living, but to council and guide the sitting Pope. It is rare, but not unheard of, for someone other than the Holy Father to see them. I have. Others have, as well. Can you describe him?"

William explained, "Well, he was old. If I had to guess, I would say in his 80s. He shuffled a little as he walked, but still seemed full of life. He had a cheery laugh and talked plainer than I would have expected..."

Cristobal interrupted, "Let me stop you right there. The cheery laugh was a dead giveaway. I have one question. Did he talk to you in Italian or English?"

"Well, English, with only a hint of an Italian accent."

"That would make sense. William, you sat here and had a conversation with Alexander VI. He has been gone from this world for almost 100 years. I am almost sure it was him. I have talked with him before, as well. Most of those who have spent any significant time inside the Basilica have, or thought they have seen him. What is unique for you is, he granted Spain the right to explore the New World. That just happens to be where you are going."

30

Days blended into weeks, and weeks transformed into months. The passage of time brought about many things. The first hint of crisp fall air on the breeze that blew through the Vatican hallways. The migration of the swallows from the north, toward the Mediterranean to the south. The arrival of the Roman festival of Cerelia and accompanying feast, something William found he struggled to stay away from. The variety of tastes were exquisite, and overwhelming, to a man who grew up on simple meats, potatoes, and greens, with the occasional fresh catch from the North Sea. Ainslee expressed a concern that if there were many more of these festivals, they would need a bigger bed. William didn't see any possible way he was gaining weight, no matter how many meals of rich pasta and sauces he ate. Every night he, and a cavalcade of others, walked miles into the city or countryside, to tend to their flock from the spiritual realm.

The most notable event of all was a quick meeting with Pope Benedict XIV. It wasn't a conversation like the one he and Pope Alexander VI had had that night on the steps. It wasn't much of a conversation at all, just a brief shaking of hands and a momentary placing of a hand on William's head, as he said a blessing.

What didn't arrive with the passage of time was a sense of comfort and relief from the events that had happened that night in the cardinal's room, and what had happened just moments before that, in his own room. He spent many hours pondering the conversation he had on the steps that night. Even if his spiritual visitor was right, it didn't mean that his wife could bear the burden of what they were asked to do.

William took every opportunity to talk to Ainslee about what he had learned and experienced. Over dinner, long walks through the streets of Rome, or just sitting in their room. He wanted to make sure she had a clear understanding of what they were in for. He never asked her if it was too much for her, or if she wanted to go home. Inside, he hoped she would say it on her own. But with each story he told her, she responded the same way, "We will go through this together." The strength he saw in her eyes was admirable, and even added to his own, but he feared it was misguided. There was no way, even with how he had explained it, that she could have an accurate understanding of all this. It was all beyond human understanding, unless you lived it as he did.

Hearing about William's concern and fears for her, Cristobal made a suggestion and included her in several of their lessons and field work, that is what William called their trips out of the Vatican to practice. After the shock, and several fainting spells, wore off, the comprehension and understanding set in. To her credit, and William's relief, she never expressed any concern or fear. Instead, she was curious, and wanted to learn along with her husband.

The day finally came where Cristobal and William sat at a table, the same table in the library that they had sat at for the last ninety three days, and the lesson ended with no other book, no other document, nothing sitting on the table next to them. The two sat in silence for several moments before he said, "You now know all that we know on this topic. You could probably teach someone yourself, and one day, God willing, you will teach your own children."

William would admit he knew more than he had when he arrived, but an expert, oh no, he felt anything but. Another question pushed that thought aside to be handled another day. It was added to the now growing list of topics for worry and consideration later. The new question had an immediacy, "What's next?"

"Well, no more training, at least not here. You will be sent to your assigned location to, quite simply, perform your duties. For you, that location is around a small area in the Colony of Virginia in the New World. I have arranged, with the help of His Holiness, for passage on a ship of settlers leaving from a port close to my home. It departs next week. Now, they can't take you straight to the colonies, the English won't allow that, but they will take you to St. Augustine, the most northern port in the Spanish territory of Florida. The local priest that will aid you will meet you there and take you north to Virginia."

"Virginia?", William asked. The question was directed more at himself than anyone else in the room. He had heard of the colonies, who hadn't? But he didn't know any of their names.

"I think you will like it there. From what I hear, the weather is a lot like what you are used to in Scotland. The dirt is dark black and rich with nutrients, perfect for farming. In fact, a small spot of land has already been secured for your family, and a small farmhouse is waiting for you."

"For us?", he asked. He wasn't asking why they were worthy of such a gift. That was not the question. Three months. It had only been a little over three months since they'd arrived at the Vatican. How was it possible that word of them had made it to the colonies in that short period of time?

"Well, yes, in a way. The farm has been there waiting for us to find the person or family that would serve the area. That William, is you and Ainslee."

William felt dumbfounded. Their simple life of just a few months past had consisted of waking up to the sounds of a rooster's crow or cow's moo. Days spent tending to the livestock, or working in the field, was a routine that was only interrupted by a trip to town to sell produce or purchase feed. Now they are doted on like they are some kind of foreign royalty on an official state visit. Neither of them have had to prepare a meal or clean their residence since they'd arrived. Now it is taking another turn, they are heading to the New World. A term William had heard many a person back home say with a sense of wonderment and fascination, without knowing what it really was. It was the promise. The promise of a new start.

Cristobal stacked the books and documents he had referred to during today's lesson, so they could be placed back on the shelves. William sat at the table with an almost dreamy look in his eyes.

"Oh, there is one more thing," Cristobal stated.

William couldn't imagine what more there could be, so he asked, "What is that?"

"Your travel papers and land are under the name of Meyer. We changed your name so that the local governors couldn't trace you back to us in any way. They won't take well with us placing someone in the leadership of a town. Might see it as tampering."

"Wait, what do you mean by leadership?"

"You will be one of the town elders of Miller's Crossing, Virginia."

31

William sat outside on his porch. His muscles ached, but it was a good ache. From hours working rows of green leafy tobacco plants that spanned across four acres of fields. This was not a crop he had ever seen before he arrived in Virginia, but with help from the neighboring farmers, he found the native plant took quite well to the dark soil. It wasn't the only crop on his property. William and Ainslee, with the help of some hired hands, had carved out a half acre adjacent to the house and set up a livestock pen and a row of plantings, just for them, or that was how it started out. It wasn't long before William shared the greens, potatoes, and parsley he grew with everyone. A little touch from their old home, for their new home. At night, William could close his eyes and let the smell of the parsley, wafting in with the sounds of the livestock, take him back to his old farm, if only just for a moment. A moment that was often interrupted by the cry of his infant son, Carl, from the other room, or a question from his oldest, Edward. The sounds of their voices would always bring him back here, the farmhouse built for them, and transformed into their home when he and Ainslee had arrived.

Cristobal, was right about this place being similar. The trees, hills, and rolling green meadows reminded him of Scotland, but it was much warmer. Occasionally, he would wake up to a layer of fog hanging over the land, but it was not the same cool marine fog that rolled in every morning and every night back home. Not that William was complaining. He had become quite used to not feeling chilled to the bone. On summer nights like tonight, after the sun went down and the most devious demon he had encountered since arriving, mosquitoes, were gone, he found peace and solace sitting out on his porch and looking up at the stars, like he had at the Vatican. Sometimes Ainslee sat out there with him. Sometimes Edward did. Ainslee would just hold his hand and gaze along with him. Edward, on the other hand, was full of questions, but one particular question was asked more than the others. "Dad, what is out there?"

Each time William would only say, "I don't know, son." Which was the truth, no matter how many times he sat there looking into the void, and past the twinkling stars, he still couldn't see that place everyone assumed was there, or the being that created and watched over the universe. It didn't make him doubt they were there. There were plenty of examples of their presence in his life.

"Ainslee?" he called from the front porch. The screen door to the porch squeaked as it opened and the hair on William's arms stood up from the gooseflesh that had developed on his arms. When Ainslee stepped out on the porch, her husband was standing up. He leaned against the railing and peered into the darkness that surrounded their home. The sun had just gone down behind the tree line. Even the last glint of green light that occurred just as the sun crossed behind the horizon was gone, leaving just the dark of night until the light raced around the globe and came up on the other side the next morning.

"Keep the youngins inside," said William. He descended the steps off the porch as he heard Ainslee usher Edward inside. He only protested a few times, asking "why" or saying he wanted to go with his dad. William's hand reached into the pocket of his brown cotton pants and pulled out a simple cross made of wood. He held it firmly in his strong and callused hands, traces of dirt from the day's work still under his nails. He disappeared into the emptiness thinking, "One day you will, son. One day you will."

Also by David Clark

You can find the next book in the series Miller's Crossing Book 2, an International Best Seller, "The Ghosts of Miller's Crossing", here.

DAVID CLARK

THE GHOSTS OF MILLER'S CROSSING

1

"This room needs some color," Edward Meyer said. The old leak stains on the white drop ceiling and scuffs on the floor were the only signs of character. The simple plastic white chair Edward sat on resembled one you might find on an outdoor patio. This was in contrast to the stainless-steel table bolted to the floor and the large two-way mirror on the wall in front of him.

He mumbled with a chuckle, "Looks slightly institutional to me," then remembered he needed to be careful. You never knew when someone might be watching.

Today was his eighteenth birthday and he sat alone in a green cotton shirt, drawstring pants, and slippers. This was no birthday celebration. He was there for an important discussion with his doctor. In truth, it was more of an evaluation; one he had high hopes for.

He thought about the first time he waited, alone, in this room. The table and chair were the same, but his attire and reason for being there was different. He wore jeans and an Iron Maiden t-shirt and sat there confused as to why he was there. He was only fourteen, and things had been rough with his foster parents. OK, "rough" might not be the best word. "Horrendous," yeah, that's the correct term. He wasn't beaten or neglected. Food, care, clothes, etc... nothing was withheld. In fact, to those looking in from the outside, he'd had a great childhood with supportive foster parents that gave him all they could to make sure he had a wonderful loving home.

When he turned nine, they encouraged him to sign up for little league, which he jumped at. He loved baseball. They traveled around to every practice and game, ensuring he always saw two parents supporting him. The same for every school event. To some extent, he felt they were trying to overcompensate for him having lost both parents in a horrible tragedy at age seven.

The door clicked and Edward saw the tall, slender forty-something frame of Doctor Law enter. His nose buried in papers as always.

"Good morning, Edward." Doctor Law said. His name was always the source of a few jokes among Edward and the other patients. *With a name like that, he should be a lawyer.* But Edward's favorite was, *he was the "Law" around this place.* He liked that one, because it was true, and it was his joke.

Doctor Law pulled a chair away from the table, and then stopped with a bewildered look on his face. He frantically studied the folder in his hands. Without looking up he said, "I will be right back. I have the wrong folder." He walked back out the door, flipping through the pages with the look of confusion growing the whole time.

Edward always wondered if these types of mistakes were legitimate or some kind of experiment, with someone observing the subject's reactions through the two-way portal in the wall. He played it cool, sat, and waited for the doctor to return.

The two-way mirror grabbed his attention during his first visit as well. They didn't hide what it was, just who was behind it. He remembered sitting there, focusing as hard as he could to see through it; hoping his foster parents were on the other side and would be in soon to take him home. That was not the case. Instead, only Doctor Law entered the room.

They talked for hours about many topics. He asked about his relationship with his foster mom, and then about his foster father. To both questions, Edward gave glowing answers about how close he felt to them and how great his life was going.

The conversation moved to school and friends. He wanted to know if Edward was being bullied or harassed at school. He suggested that kids sometimes single out a child who has been in a foster home or has had a traumatic past. Well, the answer to that was most definitely not. Edward had lots of friends, both in and away from school. Other than the normal ribbing you give each other during a baseball game or in the schoolyard, he remembered nothing like bullying. He couldn't think of any time he may have bullied anyone else, either.

Doctor Law asked him if any of his friends tried to get him to take or experiment with any kind of drugs. That answer was a very loud, "Absolutely not!" His foster parents asked him about drugs once before too. They even took him to the doctor for testing. Edward tried everything he could to convince them. Two days later, the results were in, and his foster parents were apologetic. They explained they heard rumors from other parents about drug use among his friends, and wanted to be sure. Doctor Law listened to his answer while consulting a file laid out on the table before him. He didn't challenge Edward's answer, or ask him any more questions about it.

Next, he asked about his real parents. Edward thought for a minute about how to answer, since he was still unsure why he was there. He could have said he never thought about them or what happened to them anymore, but that would have been a lie. He thought about it daily. Sometimes hourly. He told Doctor Law how he felt, and how bad he missed them. Edward then felt the need to explain. He loved his foster parents, but he missed his real parents. Doctor Law interrupted his explanation to tell him that was normal, and they understood that. Hearing that made Edward feel less guilty, though it was not really bothering him much.

Doctor Law asked delicately about the moment he found them. Edward shifted in his seat and explained, "Something woke me up. I laid there for a few moments and heard several loud crashes coming from the kitchen. I called for my mom and she never answered. I heard another crash, and she screamed. I walked downstairs and pushed open the door. That's when... I saw both lying on the floor." Edward sighed heavily. "Shortly after that a police officer came in and rushed me out of the house."

This was a memory Edward wished he could lose. For months, he woke up screaming as the image of his dead parents invaded his sleep. His foster mother would storm in and hold him for hours, trying with all her might to protect him from the memory, but nothing drove it away.

Moments after Edward walked in, Officer Tillingsly grabbed and rushed him out to his patrol car. He left him there for the longest minute or two of his life. When he returned, he took Edward to the police station. The officer was a friend of Edward's father, and was always around. He could tell Officer Tillingsly was in as much shock as Edward. He sat Edward in the chair behind his desk and gave him a soda to drink. Sitting in a chair beside him, they talked about anything and everything, including a fishing trip he'd taken with Edward and his father over the summer.

They'd been out there for hours with no bites, if you didn't count the bugs. Officer Tillingsly thought he had a bite on his line once. He reeled it in close to the boat, but when he looked, he leaned over the side a little too far. Flapping his arms like a back-pedaling turkey, he hung there for a few seconds until gravity won and he entered the water with a splash. Edward remember hearing his father laughing while saying, 'Well, Lewis, if we weren't going to catch anything before, we won't now. You scared them all off."

When they got home, Edward's mother asked if they caught anything. Edward told her, "We caught Officer Tillingsly." She looked at them like they had lost their minds. All three busted out in hysterical laughter. There was no laughter between them this time. His attempt to distract Edward—both of them really—failed.

The station itself was a hive of activity. Everyone moved around from one room to another in a blur. All talking, and all giving Edward the same heartbroken look as they walked past. Some even had tears in their eyes. Everyone, and I mean everyone, knew his family in this typical small town with only one elementary, junior, and senior high school. On top of that, his father was a local legend. He was a high school All-American Quarterback. Sportswriters and scouts came from all over to meet him during his senior year. He had the pick of prime offers from the best schools, and I do mean the best schools. Alabama, Penn State, and Notre Dame were at the top of a long list. Even with all those great offers, he bypassed college to stay and work the family farm.

After high school, he married his high school sweetheart. They were both active in the community, helping to run the fall festival each year, things at church, town council meetings, and the school board. With all of that, Edward's house was always full of the sounds of laughter and conversation. Most memories were happy ones, but there were a few that were not so joyous. Once or twice a month, a group of men would show up late at night and talk to his father for a few minutes before leaving. Edward would hear a car door close when he came home the next morning just before sunrise. His parents never discussed what this was about in front of him; all he knew was that his father kept to himself and seemed different for the next couple of days.

A click from the door gave Edward the sense of déjà vu, as Doctor Law opened the door carrying a file like he did about ten minutes ago. He hoped it is the right file this time. He sat back in his chair and watched the doctor circle around to the only other chair in the room. Edward cleared his mind; it was now time for his Oscar-worthy performance.

Want more Miller's Crossing? Check out the Miller's Crossing series?

Miller's Crossing Book 1 – The Ghosts of Miller's Crossing – Available Now
Amazon US
Amazon UK

Ghosts and demons openly wander around the small town of Miller's Crossing. Over 250 years ago, the Vatican assigned a family to be this town's "keeper" to protect the realm of the living from their "visitors". There is just one problem. Edward Meyer doesn't know that is his family, yet.

Tragedy struck Edward twice. The first robbed him of his childhood and the truth behind who and what he is. The second, cost him his wife, sending him back to Miller's Crossing to start over with his two children.

What he finds when he returns is anything but what he expected. He is thrust into a world that is shocking and mysterious, while also answering and great many questions. With the help of two old friends, he rediscovers who and what he is, but he also discovers another truth, a dark truth. The truth behind the very tragedy that took so much from him. Edward faces a choice. Stay, and take his place in what destiny had planned for him,or run, leaving it and his family's legacy behind.

Miller's Crossing Book 2 – The Demon of Miller's Crossing – Available for Pre-Order
Amazon US
Amazon UK

The people of Miller's Crossing believed the worst of the "Dark Period" they had suffered through was behind them, and life had returned to normal. Or, as normal as life can be in a place where it is normal to see ghosts walking around. What they didn't know was the evil entity that tormented them was merely lying in wait.

After a period of thirty dark years, Miller's Crossing had now enjoyed eight years of peace and calm, allowing the scars of the past to heal. What no one realizes is under the surface the evil entity that caused their pain and suffering is just waiting to rip those wounds open again. Its instrument for destruction will be an unexpected, familiar, and powerful force in the community.

Prequel – The Origins of Miller's Crossing – Available Now
Amazon US
Amazon UK

There are six known places in the world that are more "spectrally" active than anywhere else. The Vatican has taken care to assign "sensitives" and "keepers" to each of those to protect the realm of the living from the realm of the dead. With the colonization of the New World, a seventh location has been found, and time for a new recruit.

William Miller is a simple farmer in the 18th century coastal town of St. Margaret's Hope Scotland. His life is ordinary and mundane, mostly. He does possess one unique skill. He sees ghosts.

A chance discovery of his special ability exposes him to an organization that needs people like him. An offer is made, he can stay an ordinary farmer, or come to the Vatican for training to join a league of "sensitives" and "keepers" to watch over and care for the areas where the realm of the living and the dead interaction. Will he turn it down, or will he accept and prove he has what it takes to become one of the true legends of their order? It is a decision that can't be made lightly, as there is a cost to pay for generations to come.

ALSO BY DAVID CLARK

Want more frights?

Ghost Storm – Available Now

Amazon US

Amazon UK

There is nothing natural about this hurricane. An evil shaman unleashes a super-storm powered by an ancient Amazon spirit to enslave to humanity. Can one man realize what is important in time to protect his family from this danger?

Successful attorney Jim Preston hates living in his late father's shadow. Eager to leave his stress behind and validate his hard work, he takes his family on a lavish Florida vacation. But his plan turns to dust when a malicious shaman summons a hurricane of soul-stealing spirits.

Though his skeptical lawyer mind disbelieves at first, Jim can't ignore the warnings when the violent wraiths forge a path of destruction. But after numerous unsuccessful escape attempts, his only hope of protecting his wife and children is to confront an ancient demonic force head-on... or become its prisoner.

Can Jim prove he's worth more than a fancy house or car and stop a brutal spectral horde from killing everything he holds dear?

Have you read them all?

Game Master Series

Book One - Game Master – Game On

This fast-paced adrenaline filled series follows Robert Deluiz and his friends behind the veil of 1's and 0's and into the underbelly of the online universe where they are trapped as pawns in a sadistic game show for their very lives. Lose a challenge, and you die a horrible death to the cheers and profit of the viewers. Win them all, and you are changed forever.

Can Robert out play, outsmart, and outlast his friends to survive and be crowned Game Master?

Buy book one, Game Master: Game On and see if you have what it takes to be the Game Master.

Available now on Amazon and Kindle Unlimited

Book Two - Game Master – Playing for Keeps

The fast-paced horror for Robert and his new wife, Amy, continue. They think they have the game mastered when new players enter with their own set of rules, and they have no intention of playing fair. Motivated by anger and money, the root of all evil, these individuals devise a plan a for the Robert and his friends to repay them. The price... is their lives.

Game Master Play On is a fast-paced sequel ripped from today's headlines. If you like thriller stories with a touch of realism and a stunning twist that goes back to the origins of the Game Master show itself, then you will love this entry in David Clark's dark web trilogy, Game Master.

Buy book two, Game Master: Playing for Keeps to find out if the SanSquad survives.

Available now on Amazon and Kindle Unlimited

Book Three - Game Master – Reboot

With one of their own in danger, Robert and Doug reach out to a few of the games earliest players to mount a rescue. During their efforts, Robert finds himself immersed in a Cold War battle to save their friend. Their adversary... an ex-KGB super spy, now turned arms dealer, who is considered one of the most dangerous men walking the planet. Will the skills Robert has learned playing the game help him in this real world raid? There is no trick CGI or trap doors here, the threats are all real.

Buy book three, Game Master: Reboot to read the thrilling conclusion of the Game Master series.

Available now on Amazon and Kindle Unlimited

Highway 666 Series

Book One – Highway 666

A collection of four tales straight from the depths of hell itself. These four tales will take you on a high-speed chase down Highway 666, rip your heart out, burn you in a hell, and then leave you feeling lonely and cold at the end.

Stories Include:

- Highway 666 - The fate of three teenagers hooked into a demonic ride-share.
- Till Death – A new spin on the wedding vows
- Demon Apocalypse - It is the end of days, but not how the Bible described it.
- Eternal Journey - A young girl is forever condemned to her last walk, her journey will never end

Available now on Amazon and Kindle Unlimited

Book Two – The Splurge

A collection of short stories that follows one family through a dysfunctional Holiday Season that makes the Griswold's look like a Norman Rockwell painting.

Stories included:

- Trick or Treat – The annual neighborhood Halloween decorating contest is taken a bit too far and elicits some unwilling volunteers.
- Family Dinner – When your immediate family abandons you on Thanksgiving, what do you do? Well, you dig down deep on the family tree.
- The Splurge – This is a "Purge" parody focused around the First Black Friday Sale.
- Christmas Eve Nightmare – The family finds more than a Yule log in the fireplace on Christmas Eve

Available now on Amazon and Kindle Unlimited

WHAT DID YOU THINK OF THE ORIGINS OF MILLER'S CROSSING?

First of all, thank you for purchasing *The Origins of Miller's Crossing*. I know you could have picked any number of books to read, but you picked this book and for that I am extremely grateful.

I hope that it provided you a few moments of enjoyment. If so, it would be really nice if you could share this book with your friends and family by posting to [Facebook](#) and [Twitter](#).

If you enjoyed this book and found some benefit in reading this, I'd like to hear from you and hope that you could take some time to post a review on Amazon. Your feedback and support will help this author to greatly improve his writing craft for future projects and make this book even better.

You can follow this link to [The Origins of Miller's Crossing](#) now.

GET YOUR FREE READERS KIT

Subscribe to David Clark's Reader's Club and in addition to all the news, updates, and special offers available to members, you will receive a free book just for joining.
Get Yours Now! - https://mailchi.mp/8d8c7323151e/davidclarkhorror

ABOUT THE AUTHOR

David Clark is an author of multiple self-published thriller novellas and horror anthologies (amazon genre top 100) and can be found in 3 published horror anthologies. His writing focuses on the thriller and suspense genre with shades toward horror and science fiction. His writing style takes a story based on reality, develops characters the reader can connect with and pull for, and then sends the reader on a roller-coaster journey the best fortune teller could not predict. He feels his job is done if the reader either gasps, makes a verbal reaction out loud, throws the book across the room, or hopefully all three.

You can follow him on social media.
Facebook - https://www.facebook.com/DavidClarkHorror
Twitter - @davidclark6208

The Origins of Miller's Crossing © 2020 by David Clark. All Rights Reserved.

All rights reserved. No part of this book may be reproduced in any form or by any electronic or mechanical means including information storage and retrieval systems, without permission in writing from the author. The only exception is by a reviewer, who may quote short excerpts in a review.

Cover designed by Kritzel Kunst
Edited by Tamra Crow

This book is a work of fiction. Names, characters, places, and incidents either are products of the author's imagination or are used fictitiously. Any resemblance to actual persons, living or dead, events, or locales is entirely coincidental.

David Clark
Visit my website at www.facebook.com/davidclarkhorror

Printed in the United States of America

First Printing: May 2020
Frightening Future Publishing

ISBN-13 979-8638231392

This book is dedicated to my buddy, my friend, my dog Chip. He was always there to listen to me, no matter what I was talking about and never complained. Instead he gave unconditional love. Your loss has affected me more than I ever expected, but your life has enriched mine in ways I will never be able to explain. I will never forget you.

Printed in Great Britain
by Amazon